ISLINGTON

D1765647

Please return this item on or before the last date s
be liable to overdue charges. To renew an item ca
access the online catalogue at www.islington.gov.
your library membership number and PIN number.

9/16

1 5 OCT 2016

2 MAR 2017

1 8 MAR 2017

10/24 AL

Islington Libraries

020 7527 6900   **www.islington.gov.uk/libraries**

Diversion Books
A Division of Diversion Publishing Corp.
443 Park Avenue South, Suite 1008
New York, New York 10016
www.DiversionBooks.com

For more information, email info@diversionbooks.com

First Diversion Books edition May 2016.
Print ISBN: 978-1-68230-082-4
eBook ISBN: 978-1-68230-081-7

"Everyone has a story."
—Sierra Dark

CHAPTER ONE

Emma Glass was late to work, thanks to her two German shepherd puppies—as yet unnamed—who had decided they weren't ready to be left without adoring companionship. So she called her best friend, Jenny Wright, over to babysit the new fur babies while she went to the clinic. Asking your best friend to watch your pets the day after Thanksgiving was no small thing, but Jenny agreed with a squeal and said she could study case law while she kept an eye on Emma's pet menagerie: the pups, her high-minded blue-point Persian Princess, and her two beautiful lovebirds.

Disorganized seemed to be the catchword of the day. Emma stuffed her red hair up in a bird's nest, brushed her teeth, and hurried out the door.

She shifted her very old green Jeep, turning into the parking lot of the sole vet clinic in Star Canyon, New Mexico, which had been run by her father before her, and which she'd taken over last year after her father had passed away. The last three years she'd had the pleasure of working at the clinic with him, learning under him, and getting to know her patients.

The low-slung brown building that housed the clinic always felt like a second home to her, her father's presence all around.

Parking in the last spot in the employee section around back, she got out, stuck her feet in her rubber work shoes, and slipped her black backpack over her shoulder. Very urban, Jenny called the backpack, which had made Emma laugh, because they lived in a two-stoplight town of five hundred people. She grabbed up the paper sack of old, soft towels someone had kindly left on her porch as a donation for the clinic, and hurried toward the back door.

"Oof!" Something large careened into her back, sending her sailing. The concrete parking lot was cold and hard, and remnants of snow clung to her jeans, but the sweet brown eyes in a golden-furred face charmed her instantly. "Hello, handsome! If you wanted attention, you could have just said so, Joe. I love the new camo bandana. Very big-boy."

She got to her knees, felt a strong hand haul her to her feet. She was pulled up against a strong, wide chest she had dreamed of being acquainted with for years, even back to high school when she'd spent all her time studying to get a college scholarship and he'd spent his time being the local rodeo star. Santana Dark brushed her clothes off and set her back on her feet. "I'm sorry as hell, Emma. Are you all right?"

"I'm fine. Happens all the time when you work in a vet clinic." Her eyes seemed glued—and traitorously so—to Santana's tight backside as he picked up the towels, stuffed them back into the bag, and handed it to her.

He grinned. "Joe doesn't know his own strength."

"So your sister introduced you to Joe." She looked up at Santana, wishing she didn't sound so breathless. But she was, and it wasn't from getting knocked to the ground by a rambunctious seventy-pound junior golden retriever. "I didn't know you were back from Afghanistan."

He smiled, eating her up with his eyes, the way every woman said he made them feel. Emma begged her heart to quit racing.

"Got back last night. Sierra said I had dog duty right off the bat because Joe needed to come see his friend and guardian angel, Dr. Glass." He tugged lightly at a strand of Emma's hair, which had exploded from its bird's nest knot when she'd fallen. "You'd be surprised how often I thought about this crazy ruby-colored hair of yours while I was overseas."

She stepped back, gripping the bag of towels to her. "Why?"

He shrugged. "I don't really know."

Well, there it was. Just typical non-meaningful flirtation from one of the Dark brothers. The four of them—Luke, Cisco, Santana, and Romero—were all sex on a stick, and the women in Star Canyon had been trying to tie them down for years, with no success.

"I'm actually late, so I better get inside." She edged away from Joe's tongue, eagerly trying to connect with her hand in a plea for more attention. "Glad you're home safely, Santana. Bye, Joe." She relented with a swift pat for Joe as she scurried inside the clinic, away from the fiercely sexy combo of a SEAL and his dog.

Sierra had said Santana would need a friend when he

got home, and adopted Joe on the spot, the day he'd been brought in, found dumped in Star Canyon. Sierra had also said it would keep her brother from lodging his head too far up his butt once he returned, so he'd "have something else to think about besides military crap."

That was Sierra—always working an angle, keeping her brothers from getting too comfortable out at their two-thousand-acre ranch.

Emma walked past the receptionist desk, handed Connie Merritt the bag of donated towels, and tossed her backpack into her office.

"You're late," Connie said, following her. "Don't think I didn't notice Santana Dark's truck parked out front and him taking that big lug of a dog around back for a potty break. What happened to your jeans?"

Emma glanced down, spying the small tear. "Nothing."

Connie grinned. "He's been trying to get your clothes off of you for years."

"Who?"

Connie laughed and went back to her desk. "Ever thought about letting him?" she called back.

That was the trouble with your receptionist being an old friend of the family—helpful advice got ladled out often. "You're assuming I'd want him taking my clothes off." She flipped on lights in the first exam room, made sure the trays were out and clean for her first patient. The waiting room had filled pretty quickly—she'd spied two cats in carriers, Mrs. Sanders and her Chihuahua, Betty, and little Marty Johnson with his guinea pig, Squeakers. No sign of Joe and his new hunky dad, which would give her a chance to get settled into professional mode before she had to face Santana in the confines of a small examining room.

Whew.

"First patient of the day," Connie said, too cheerful for words, as she ushered Joe and Santana in.

Joe made a beeline for Emma. His master lounged against the wall, his arms crossed over his chest, slightly amused.

"Like a bull in a china shop, and a helluva welcome-home gift from my kid sister," Santana said. "So, who's been trying to get your clothes off of you for years?" He laughed at Emma's embarrassed expression. "Connie's voice carries."

It was true. Which meant the entire waiting room had heard their conversation, and no doubt everyone knew Connie had meant Santana—or they would within the next five minutes once Connie filled in the details to all very interested parties. "You know Connie. She talks a lot."

"I thought she might have been talking about me. It's not entirely true, but it wouldn't be entirely false either."

Emma's heart thundered. "Big talk coming from a man who hasn't been in Star Canyon much in years." She took a fast peep at the big-shouldered man casually eying her. Big brown eyes with long dark lashes. Sheepskin jacket, brown Stetson. Well-worn boots, great smile in a deeply tanned face. She was staring, and he'd noticed. She got Joe square on the silver table, pushed the button to raise the table to exam height, ignored Santana's grin, and hoped she wasn't blushing.

"Hello, you big baby," she crooned to Joe, who offered her a paw. "New trick?" she asked, shaking his paw and slipping him a treat.

"Sierra claims she's been working with him. Was it your idea to send this overly large hound out to our ranch?"

Thankfully they were off the dangerous topic of clothing removal. "The idea was all Sierra's. She said you'd need a friend when you got home."

"My sister loves thinking she rules the roost."

He didn't seem too worried about that, so Emma went back to checking Joe over. "You've put on six pounds since I saw you last," she told Joe, running her hands over his wiggly body. "Good boy."

"Joe got a steak last night for dinner."

Emma raised a brow. "You feed him steak?"

"He took the steak. Raw, before it hit the grill." Santana laughed. "In the future, I won't underestimate his reach."

"A little steak never hurt anyone, but don't make a habit of that, young man." She peeked in Joe's ears, nodding with satisfaction. "You're on the mend, buddy. No more infection, and according to your last stool sample, no more worms. Your blood test came back heartworm negative, which is excellent." She moved the table down, and Joe jumped off with delight, wagging his tail. "Thanks for bringing him in. I'd hoped to see improvement, and my faith has been rewarded."

"You didn't think Sierra would let any animal live a completely unpampered life, did you?"

"Exactly why I allowed him to go to the Dark ranch as opposed to the six other people who offered to adopt Joe. I know your sister and your brothers have soft hearts."

Santana looked at her. "I notice you didn't mention my soft heart."

A strange feeling hit her. It was the way he looked at her,

studying her, like he was searching for an answer to which she didn't know the question. "There's nothing soft about you, Santana, but I think everyone in this town would say that you and all your family serve your country and are good to Star Canyon." She closed up Joe's folder, opened the door. "It's good to see you again. Both of you." Emma gave Joe one last fond pat and headed into the hallway.

"Connie's right about me, you know," he murmured as he stepped into the hall, way too close for comfort. So very close, so tall and strong. He even smelled sexy, like clean, warm, manly skin, and she concentrated on keeping her distance. Not looking like she was falling under a spell. Emma thanked her lucky stars for Connie's curious gaze and the full waiting room also staring at them with great interest so she could escape into the next examining room.

"I have a guinea pig patient, and by the squeals I hear, mini-Marty is none too happy to be in an establishment with cats. Good-bye, Santana."

She hurried into waiting room 2 to the sound of Santana's deep chuckle, her heart beating way too hard. Oh, who was she kidding?

She was crazy about Santana Dark. So many muscles, so much attitude.

But taking on that much heat—well, there was no reason for her to desert her geeky-girl origins. There was plenty of attraction between her and Santana, but attraction was nothing solid to build a relationship on. Or build anything on. The Dark men, every last one of them, had never been engaged and never pretended to be interested in matrimony. For that matter, Emma wasn't exactly known for the longevity of her relationships. A few boyfriends scattered throughout college and one in vet school that might have turned serious if she hadn't decided to return to Star Canyon. She'd made the right decision—knowing in her heart that she didn't feel about any man the way she'd always felt about Santana. And it wasn't something she could solely ascribe to unrequited youthful longings. Somehow she'd always known he meant more to her than any other man.

She sternly commanded her blood to quit racing and the parts of her body which had no business heating to cool off. The very last thing she needed to do was drool after Star Canyon's most elusive bachelor, now that he'd finally returned home—for however long.

• • •

Sierra glared at him when Santana walked into the big, roomy kitchen, a little in need of updating but still the cozy place they'd always gathered for meals. This was home, and he'd missed the hell out of it in a way he was just now beginning to understand. Here this rambling ranch house, surrounded by miles of fields and pasture, was his touchstone. Everything he'd learned about being a strong, loyal person, deeply committed to family and community, he'd learned from his parents raising them in this house.

"Where's Joe?" his bossy baby sister demanded.

"Outside taking in some fresh air."

"He should be with you at all times."

Santana edged into a ladder-back chair and gave his sister a stern eying. "Did you get Joe for me so that I'd have to go to the vet clinic to see Emma?"

"Of course not!" She didn't meet his eyes. "I got Joe

because I knew you'd come home with all kinds of mental problems, the same mental problems you had before you left." She looked thoroughly pleased with herself. "Joe needed a friend, and you need a friend. One plus one equals two good buddies who need each other."

"I think you sent me up there just so I'd have to be in a small room with Emma." Which had been a pretty good plan, actually. Seeing Emma again, watching her calmly and capably taking care of her patients, had put her squarely on his mind. He stopped his sister's cleaning of the kitchen table by removing the rag from her hands. "I smelled a rat when Connie told me Joe didn't have an appointment."

"Oh, pooh." Sierra shrugged. "Of course he had an appointment. Didn't Joe get seen?"

"Yes. First patient of the day. Which was also strange, given that there was a waiting room full of cats, dogs, and guinea pigs, and somehow, we got to see the pretty doctor first."

Sierra smiled at him. "How nice of Connie to fit you in. I mean, fit Joe in."

"You're not doing this very well." If there was one thing he knew about his sister, it was that she was a first-rate buttinski, rushing headlong where angels feared to tread, pushing her older brothers around because she knew she could get away with it.

Usually. Not this time.

"I'll manage my own love life, thanks."

She sent him a sidelong glance and snatched the rag away. "Go away. You're bothering me. Go teach Joe to fetch a tennis ball. He needs to burn off energy. And so do you."

She glanced up. "By the way, I take it as an encouraging sign that you even notice that Emma's pretty."

"Of course she's pretty." Emma was hot, with her rubber shoes and her big, friendly smile—not that she smiled at him all that much, but Joe had certainly gotten the treatment. She was sexy, always had been, but at twenty-nine, she was a full-blown woman men would look twice at, and more. Hell, even eight-year-old Marty had stared up at Emma with something akin to rapture on his little freckled face as he'd held Squeakers in a box like a trophy.

Sierra laughed. "She's too good for you, you know."

"Then why'd you send me to see her?"

"Assuming I did, which I'm not admitting to, I just thought you'd want to see what you're missing out on. Before it's gone forever."

He raised a brow. "Where's it going?"

"I don't know," Sierra said mysteriously, "but the grapevine has it that one of our esteemed Star Canyon bachelors is planning to ask her out."

Santana swallowed a growl. "Who?"

His sister smiled cagily. "I don't know."

"You know."

"Foster Smith."

He rolled his eyes. "Emma wouldn't go out with him."

Sierra didn't say anything. She opened the back door, and Joe thundered in, shaking his body and jingling his collar, then making a beeline for Santana. He patted the dog, his fingers smoothing through the thick, golden coat. "Would she?"

"On paper, Foster and Emma would be a good match. He teaches math at the high school, and Emma's something of a brainiac. He also helps coach the kids and runs an after-school program for kids whose parents work and have no place else to go. Helps them with their homework. Does any of this penetrate your thick skull, brother dearest?"

"Yeah." Santana got up. "Come on, Joe. Let's go burn off some energy with a swim."

"In thirty-two-degree weather?" Sierra demanded. "Are you missing parts of your brain?"

Maybe. Even likely. Unfortunately, all his brain wanted to do was think about Emma, now that he'd seen her again, been near that womanly body, heard her sweet voice.

The scarred, caged beast in him roared, demanding to explore the comfort of soft, gentle territory.

But freshly returned from war was no time to appease the beast. It wouldn't be fair to Emma. Four deployments, the last the worst of all. He had physical scars, of course: a couple of bullet wounds from enemy snipers, a long gash on his leg where an IED…he shut down the thoughts the beast wanted him to remember. He wouldn't think or talk about those days.

Nothing but icy-cold water was going to get Emma out of his mind now. He'd thought about her constantly overseas, and even then he couldn't have said exactly why he couldn't get her out of his mind—except for that one kiss they'd shared back in high school, courtesy of a dumb dare where Bobby Sanford had dared him to kiss the class geek because, as Bobby said, somebody had to throw himself on the pyre for the sake of mankind.

So Santana had done it—a really fast kiss in the hallway as they'd lined up for graduation, when it was too late for teachers to do anything about it if Emma got all mad at him about it. He'd pressed his lips against hers, going for a fast kiss—and to his shock, found soft, pliable lips that molded to his and sucked him in, like kissing a delicious red velvet cupcake. He'd wanted to lean into the soft moistness that was Emma's mouth so badly, but the greatest shock of all was when he felt her lips press against his in sweet response. He'd thanked his lucky stars the graduation gown covered the erection that sprang to life—and when the line of students erupted in cheers, he'd broken away, staring at her guiltily.

Emma had looked back at him, her face a little flushed, her red hair spiraling out from under the white mortar board. He'd thought she looked like an angel.

But the angel had gone off to college, and he'd gone off to enlist. The kiss had stayed on his mind. No matter how many women crossed his path, he'd never forgotten the softness of Emma's mouth.

All that sweet velvety hotness would be criminally wasted on well-meaning, upstanding-citizen Foster Smith.

CHAPTER TWO

Santana felt the presence in his room before his three oversized brothers said a word. "Don't you even think about it," he said, not bothering to open his eyes. "If you dogpile me like we did when we were kids, I promise my reaction won't be favorable."

His brothers guffawed and leaped on his bed anyway, which meant Joe, who'd slept peacefully and obediently beside his bed all night, leaped onto his bed, too.

"Welcome home, bro!" Cisco tried to rub a knot on Santana's head, and he swatted his brother's hand away.

"Sorry we didn't greet you sooner." This from Romero, who told Joe to get off the bed and quit being an attention hog.

"Never thought you'd come back home," Luke said. "Now that you're back, we have lots of work for you to do. We're presuming you'll be joining up either at the fire station or the sheriff's office, but the ranch needs another hand, too."

"Assholes, get *off*," Santana growled, secretly enjoying the brotherly camaraderie. These brothers, his family, were his reason to return. Glutton for punishment, he'd said at the time he'd left, but the truth had been that he needed to stay away then. Wasn't ready to come home to the ranch and Star Canyon. Kept thinking there was more out there he needed to do. He'd elected to do one more tour of duty because he believed in the mission and the brotherhood of his team had kept him sane.

Home felt pretty damn good, filled in a hole he hadn't known needed healing.

"Heard you asked Emma Glass out," Cisco said.

Santana abandoned his bed to the dogpile, pulled on some jeans. "That's a dumb rumor, even for Star Canyon."

"But is it true?" Luke asked. "According to the grapevine, which is white-hot over this, you practically kissed her at the clinic yesterday."

"We got probably twenty calls while we were on the road buying a couple of new horses," Romero said. "So, Emma, huh? You didn't waste any time. You've been back all of what, twenty-four hours?"

Santana shoved a worn Stetson on his head and decided now was as good a time as any to hit the chores. "Emma might have a date with someone, but it's not me. Sierra says Foster Smith is going to ask her out. Or did already. I didn't catch the details."

His brothers roared with laughter. Santana grimaced.

"Dude, Foster's not asking Emma out," Luke said. "He's getting married next weekend."

Santana glared at his brothers, then pulled on a blue long-sleeved work shirt. "Sierra said—"

They filed out of the room, shaking their heads. Cisco shot him a sympathetic look as he followed his brothers, and the look clearly said *you poor dumbass, you let Sierra sucker you again.*

Had his sister been trying to get him to realize his feelings for Emma? There was nothing Sierra liked better than to keep her brothers with their boots set firmly on *run.* He reminded himself that Sierra reveled in her position as the baby of the family, and thought her services were required to manage their lives.

"Come on," Santana said to Joe, who perked up instantly now that he realized he was the center of Santana's world again. "I smell eggs and bacon. If you lie down in the den and let me eat, I'll sneak you an egg."

Joe planted his paws on Santana's chest, his gaze delighted with the promise. "Oh, you don't know what I'm saying. You're just working an angle, dog, like everybody else around here. Get down before you hurt something. Probably me."

For a dog that was only about a year old, Joe was really big. Santana couldn't believe his sister had saddled him with a needy canine. And was trying to saddle him with a girlfriend, too, obviously. His brothers were going to try to sign him up for the fire station or the sheriff's office.

It was oddly comforting to know that Star Canyon hadn't changed at all in his absence.

• • •

Emma closed up the clinic. There'd been two surgeries, a splinter removed from a paw, assorted checkups and boo-

boos, and even a turtle that had cracked its shell. Marty had returned with Squeakers, but the sweet black-and-white guinea pig seemed to be responding well to mite treatment with special shampoo and changing to newspaper bedding.

She drove home, stopping only to grab takeout. Jenny and the two new puppies were curled up studying in the den. "I brought takeout from The Last Stop café. Hope you're hungry."

Jenny got up. "I'm hungry for gossip." She peered in the bag, pulled out bread wrapped in foil, sighed with pleasure. Dug a little deeper for the two containers of steaming pot roast and carrots. "Since you ran into Santana yesterday, I've gotten several texts saying that you two are practically an item."

"Not true. And you know it's not." Jenny kicked off her rubber shoes, then headed to her room to change and wash up. "I consider it a good sign that the puppies barely raised their heads to look at me when I came in. Busy day?"

"We played catch and tag and watch Aunt Jenny fall on her butt in the snow. The dogs liked that game the best, because then they got toweled off with soft towels. I'll put this in the oven while you change."

Emma hopped in the shower, thinking about Santana's dark eyes on her. An item? So far from it she had to marvel at Star Canyon's penchant for matchmaking. But Joe had a good home with Santana and the rest of the Dark clan, and that was all that mattered.

She hurried, not allowing herself to enjoy the unbidden fantasy of soaping Santana's strong body. Toweling off, sighing with contentment now that she was refreshed and a meal was waiting, she jumped into some comfy gray sweats, pulled her wet hair into a loose ponytail, then padded down the hall, her nose leading the way to the delicious smell of warming pot roast.

"We have company," Jenny said, grinning from ear to ear because Santana had made himself quite at home at her kitchen table, with a German shepherd puppy in his arms, another at his feet.

"I brought dinner," Santana said.

"So did I." She tried to act like Santana showing up in her kitchen was no big deal, but frankly, it was a big deal even by Star Canyon's fast-and-furious matchmaking standards.

"I brought dinner for Gus and Bean." Santana couldn't have looked sexier if he'd tried, and Emma was aware Jenny was trying not to laugh at the stunned expression on Emma's face. Big and hunky in worn blue jeans and a dark blue shirt, his gaze on hers—and what woman could resist a man who loved animals?

"Gus and Bean?" She got a sparkling water from the fridge, gulped at it, trying to cool down her suddenly very nervous libido. The sexual tension kicking in caught her off guard. At first she'd thought she was having some kind of weird hot flash, then realized the only flash she was having was a major Santana flash.

Which meant it had been way too long since she'd been kissed by a man. Really kissed—and then some.

"Your puppies." He kissed the one he held and handed him to her. "Jenny said they're called Gus and Bean."

"Sure. Why not." She hadn't named them yet because she'd just taken them in when she'd been contacted by a rescue society for veterinary care. Emma shot a glance at

Jenny, who had a distinctly pleased air about her as she took the plates of pot roast from the oven.

"There you go." Jenny looked at both of them. "I've got to scoot, kids. Early morning tomorrow, and I still have tons of studying to do. Case law really takes it out of a girl." She patted the newly christened Gus and Bean, then pulled on her coat and a red-striped muffler. "You be good boys for your mom tonight. You don't know it, but you've landed in pretty awesome digs. Welcome home, Santana." She waved at Emma and departed on a rush of cold air that gusted into the kitchen when she opened and closed the door.

Santana studied her. "I didn't really bring dinner for Gus and Bean. I brought it for us, and I think Jenny figured that out. I didn't mean to run her off."

Emma shook her head. "She'd been here all day, now that she's assigned herself chief babysitter for the puppies. I'm sure she's happy to get home. Besides, she took one of your meals."

He glanced at the huge white plastic sack he'd put on the table. "She sure did, the minx."

"Mm." Emma got up on a bar stool. "To what do I owe the honor?"

He passed her a plastic takeout dish. "Joe sends his regrets and promises he'll learn manners quickly."

She could have sat and stared at Santana all night. She'd heard he'd been a sniper, and that he'd been awarded commendations for kills. He wouldn't talk about his last deployment if she asked, so she focused on the food he'd brought. "I'll split my pot roast with you, and I'll rob you of half of Joe's offerings. I'm too starved to be polite."

"I took a chance that food would get me in the door,

so help yourself." He grinned, a charming bad boy. "I think I also owe you for a pair of jeans. Connie said yours ripped yesterday when Joe knocked you down."

"You don't owe me a thing." Emma perked up. "However, the clinic could use some things."

"You haven't changed, and I'm happy to see it."

Emma hesitated. "Of course I've changed. You've changed, too."

"No. You're still Emma, the girl with the heart of gold."

"Hardly. My heart is steel, that's all. And not too proud to beg when it comes to the clinic. Now, about a donation." She smiled, and he smiled back, warming her. "We could use some fence repair out back, because I'd like to have a genuine dog run for the dogs to get fresh air. A kennel, so they can get exercise. We have the space, but the fence isn't secure, not for the bigger dogs, and certainly not for the diggers."

"I'll get my brothers on it. It'll be done faster than you can blink."

Emma smiled. "Thank you."

"No problem. That was an easy one." He certainly didn't look all that concerned, although it was a big project. Emma decided she'd save that detail for later. No reason to scare him off.

When had Santana ever been afraid of anything?

"Anyway," Santana said, "it appears there's been plenty of gossip going around about us."

Folks in Star Canyon embellished if there weren't solid details to work with. "It'll blow over."

"That's just the thing. I'm kind of hoping it doesn't. I was going to try that theory on you, see how you feel."

Her heart kicked up uncomfortably. For some reason,

her traitorous eyes wouldn't stop staring at his nicely shaped mouth, his broad shoulders—oh, just all of him. "Why would you want to encourage gossip?"

He shrugged. "You and I will both know there's nothing to the rumors."

She *wanted* there to be something. The problem was, she was no sex kitten. This was as sexy as she got most days: springy wet hair, no makeup, rushing from home to clinic and back. She wasn't the type of woman Santana would go for. Even in high school, he'd run with a faster crowd than hers—and sexy, athletic Donna Adams with the sleek blonde hair had been his steady.

Of course, Donna had three kids now and a job at Toby Smith's Quick-Mart, so the sexy had worn off a bit. Donna was one of the sweetest people Emma knew, but back then, she'd been a little envious of Donna catching Santana's attention.

Now he was offering her a relationship of sorts—but there were dangers for her.

"So you don't want me to deny the gentle-natured ribbing and matchmaking of our friends."

"Right." He nodded. "They'll just make up something if we discourage them, and what they make up might be worse. No harm, no foul."

"You're the guy who's going to have no sex life if people have you heading to the altar with me. Fair warning."

"What about your sex life?"

"*My* sex life?" she asked. Emma straightened her shoulders, trying to look like she remembered what a sex life even was.

"Sierra told me you and Foster are kind of a thing, but

then I heard Foster's getting married soon. Catch me up on the Star Canyon news."

Emma wrinkled her nose. "Sierra told a tiny whopper."

"Tiny?"

"I'm trying to be polite."

"Ah. Good of you." He looked at her so intently she wished she was in his lap, his mouth on hers—

Whoa. Stop that, she told her frazzled, sex-deprived body.

"So you're not pining for Foster?"

"Foster and I were a thing, a while ago. Long over." She realized she'd never pined for Foster, not the way she'd pined for Santana. "He's getting married soon, and I couldn't be happier for him," she said definitely. "Foster and I were more friends than we were soul mates."

He smiled at her, and Emma felt it inside her soul. Her heart melted into a puddle of gooey mush.

"And you?" she said, hating that she asked.

"Nothing of any great interest."

Oh, damn. There was that smile again, letting her know she'd have to dig harder to get more information out of him. He wasn't going to make it easy, teasing her with mystery. He was here in her house, he'd accepted Joe with good grace, and okay, she'd always wondered if that graduation-day kiss had been that awesome, or if she'd just been innocent and shell-shocked by being kissed by Santana Dark.

They had to get off this topic. She drank some tea, deciding to go for nonchalant. "It won't matter, since we're not going to be denying any rumors, I guess."

He leaned back and grinned. "I like the sound of that. Benefits for both of us."

Benefits? She hadn't had any benefits in a long time.

"Here's the thing," Emma said, her heart racing like mad. She got up, crossed around the table, approached him. "Don't let this scare you, but—"

"Sweetheart, there's very little that scares me."

She looked into his eyes. Santana gazed back at her, completely oblivious to what her traitorous body was urging her to do. It was now or never. Her courage was tiny, a fractional small voice of daring shouting at her to get her inner sex kitten on—so Emma leaned close, placing her lips against his, closing her eyes tightly.

Felt him freeze.

She was making an ass of herself.

She gasped as he hauled her into his lap, taking her mouth with his, holding her in his big strong arms, her face held gently in his hands. Eagerly she leaned into the kiss, sighing as she felt his hands roam under the waistband of her sweats. All the lightning bolts she remembered hit her all over again, only now she wanted more. She wanted him to kiss her and never stop.

He stopped. Looked into her eyes. Carefully set her out of his lap.

"I've got to get back for chores with my brothers. But you'll have your fence by next week, and it'll be digger-proof and jumper-proof."

"Thank you." She didn't know what else to say, she was on a limb she'd never been on before. He shoved his hat on, shot a last glance her way, and went out the door.

Just like that.

Suddenly she felt like she had the day he'd kissed her at graduation, practically having heart failure because the Big Man on Campus had kissed her.

Great, a little more awkward in my life is just what I needed.

But the kiss had felt wonderful while it lasted. Sweet and gentle yet somehow demanding, his hand pressing her tight against his body as their lips met over and over. Tingles shot over her, goose-pimpling her skin.

Yet he'd torn out of her house faster than Joe could grab a steak.

She didn't have to wait for New Year's to start her list of resolutions. Right at the top of the list was to stay away from Santana Dark's sexy mouth and his hunky body. Be professional when he brought Joe to the clinic, and never, ever fall into his arms again.

CHAPTER THREE

By the weekend, Emma's clinic had a fence so escape-proof it was like the canine version of Ft. Knox—no dog was breaking in or out of the new runs. The clinic patients could exercise to their hearts' content. He'd kept his mind on Emma, and off anything to do with his family. And wasn't that the reason he'd stayed out of the country so long?

But today's meeting couldn't wait any longer. There was no ignoring the fact that their father was never coming back, his body had never been recovered.

It felt weird as hell sitting in this huge room in a sumptuous office in Albuquerque. Santana and his siblings grouped around a long, oval, mahogany table that looked like it was shined daily. Wide windows revealed the bustling city below. Santana idly wondered why their father hadn't used a less ostentatious firm to handle his estate. A local attorney in Star Canyon could have handled it, but then Santana realized that they hadn't had a lawyer there in some years. Folks always wanted to move to the bigger cities with more lucrative clients.

If they could wrap this thing up fast, maybe he could get home in time to stop by and see Emma, Gus, Bean, the cat, the whole menagerie. He'd stop by and get Joe, take him along.

The thought made him smile in spite of the sadness of the occasion. Santana realized he'd needed that, needed to know that life was going to go on, and that there was something on the other side from this wrap-up of his father's affairs.

I miss the hell out of Dad. Wish I could hear his voice one last time.

A tall man with collar-length brown hair and slightly sunburned skin was shown in by the same cute receptionist who'd ushered the Dark family into the room earlier. He wore a suit, unlike the Darks, who were mostly clad in jeans, boots, and western shirts, their normal attire. He glanced around at them, clearly feeling as out of place as they did.

"Hi," he said. "I guess this is the right room."

"You'd have to ask the lady," Santana said.

"She said this is the place." He sat at the opposite end of the table, turned his head to stare out the window. The view was pretty good, but Santana had the feeling the guy wasn't sure why he was here.

Which was a pretty damn good question. This was a private family dispersion of their father's estate. He was surprised when the man turned his head, sending a fast peek Sierra's way before focusing on the Albuquerque skyline again.

Santana glanced at Sierra. She shrugged, and rolled her

eyes in true Sierra fashion, well aware the poor bastard had just checked her out. Sierra looked beautiful in a dress with purple flowers scattered over it, her silvery hair up high in a ponytail with only a purple rubber band to hold it there.

Santana tried not to smirk when the poor guy made the mistake of turning and gawking at Sierra once more. His brothers twisted in their seats, edgy and protective. Sierra glared at the poor guy—her typical demeanor when letting men know their attention was unwelcome.

The man's ears turned a little red at the tops as he realized his error. But this time he stared back at all of them evenly, clearly not intimidated in the least.

Or if he was, he was a damn good bluffer.

Two suits hurried in, followed by two secretaries and a couple of other functionaries. Santana shrugged at his brothers, knowing they were equally surprised by the need for all these people to settle their simple, hardworking father's trust. It seemed incongruous that a man who had lived and worked as hard and without fanfare as Sonny Dark would need this type of attention.

"Hello, everyone," a tall, silver-haired man said to the room at large. "I'm Fairfax Morrow, and this is my associate, Darrow Smith."

The two men sat in the leather chairs, and their secretaries settled papers at their elbows. Santana shifted, apprehensive.

"You must be Nick Marshall, I'm guessing," Fairfax said to the stranger at the opposite end of the table.

"And you're the Dark family, then. Sierra, obviously," he said, nodding to her. "And you are?" he asked Santana.

"Santana. My brothers Romero, Cisco, and Luke."

"Fine." Fairfax studied the papers a moment, then

looked up. "Your father was a client of our firm for twenty years, and we were privileged that he trusted us."

Santana was astonished that his father had been coming here for twenty years. He could tell his siblings were as well.

"We were very sorry to hear of your father's passing. He was a wonderful man. We respected him greatly." Fairfax looked somber for a moment. "Please accept our condolences. Your father was a brave man."

Santana shifted again, nodding to show that the family appreciated his words.

"As you know, your father had your family property put into a trust, which was created ten years ago." He cleared his throat, and Santana realized Fairfax was uncomfortable. He glanced at Darrow, and noted he seemed intent on the papers before him. Neither man appeared happy, but that was the nature of their job. Santana just wanted them to get on with it so they could all leave. He glanced at Nick Marshall, realizing the man was staring at the skyline again. Like he wished he was anyplace but here. Santana knew how he felt.

"The estate, in its entirety, has been left to Nick Marshall," Fairfax said. "All its contents, all the land."

Nick's head whipped around, and Santana saw that he was stunned, as stunned as he was. Dimly he heard Sierra gasp as the words sank in.

"I don't understand," Santana said.

"Your father had a business partnership with his brother, a Nicholas Marshall," Darrow explained. "The business relationship began in the form of a loan, when Sonny Dark required a large sum of money."

"For what?" Romero demanded, and Santana was glad

to hear his brother asking the same question. His heart felt hollow, his stomach knotted tight. What the lawyer was saying was that they had no home, nothing—that wasn't possible. Their father wouldn't have cut them out of everything.

"For gambling debts," Fairfax said.

Cisco snapped, "Bullshit. Our father didn't gamble."

"He did at one time, and thought he had it beat. Transferred his appetite for the adrenaline of fast money to the commodities market, as he told us the story," Darrow said. "Lost his shirt, is how he relayed the facts to us. Soybeans and pork bellies, I believe. We can check the records—"

"This is crazy." Sierra leaped to her feet. "Dad wouldn't have left our home to a stranger!" She glared at Nick.

"Actually," Darrow said, "your father's name was not Sonny Dark. It was Santiago Quinto Marshall."

Santana leaned back in his chair. "There's a mistake. This whole story is completely false. People in our town would have known."

"Your father was a CIA operative before he married your mother," Darrow explained. "His life in Star Canyon suited him once he left that life behind. Unfortunately, he still craved excitement, and sought it in other ways. It was difficult living a life in witness protection, I imagine. At least that was the circumstance that he indicated to us, though he never directly told us he was in a witness protection program."

Santana laughed out loud. "We were a lot of things, but hiding out wasn't one of them. Dad worked his tail off, but he never…" His thought drifted away as he remembered their easygoing, though hardworking, childhood. They'd had a good, solid upbringing with a lot of love and support.

"Dad wasn't much for going out," Luke said, "but we weren't in hiding."

"It's our understanding that your father enjoyed spending time at home with his wife and family," Fairfax said. "Having a large family was a way to make a woman happy who had to endure the solitude of witness protection."

"Our parents had a happy marriage. Dad didn't have us just to make Mom happy. It's ridiculous." Sierra suddenly looked like she might cry.

"We misspoke, of course," Darrow said carefully. "Your father shared that each of you were adopted over the years, and—"

"Just a damn minute!" Santana shot to his feet. "I don't know what's going on here, but you're lying through your teeth. All anyone has to do is look at the five of us, and you can tell we're the same gene pool!"

The secretaries rushed to bring glasses to the table, putting one beside each of them. Santana wanted to toss his through the huge windows overlooking Albuquerque. "For obvious reasons," Fairfax said, when everyone had a drink, "your father didn't want you to know this until after his death. Keeping his family together was paramount for Sonny. Which is why ultimately he opted to go to his brother for help."

Sierra began to cry. Santana was shocked, as were his brothers. He couldn't remember ever seeing her like this. She could be sad, she could be wistful, but the deep, shuddering sobs that racked her now spoke to the bone-deep pain he would have given his arm to shield her from, as would his brothers. The secretaries went into action again with tissue and more wine, which they poured in Sierra's glass, but to

Santana's great astonishment, Nick Marshall got to his feet and handed Sierra a white handkerchief.

It had his initials embroidered in black on one side and right then, he knew that Nick Marshall had grown up quite differently than the Darks had.

"Thank you," Sierra said, handing it back to him. "If you don't mind, and not to be rude, but I don't want anything from you. Ever."

"I understand," Nick said, taking himself back to his seat. He turned his entire body to face the skyline now, not just his head. Luke and Romero comforted their sister from their seats next to her.

Santana expelled a heavy breath from the depths of his tense body. "I assume you're sure of this. And are convinced Dad was of sound mind."

"We are," Fairfax said gravely. "Absolutely. Your father's estate is worth somewhere in the neighborhood of five million dollars, thanks to land appreciation largely. He was very careful to make certain that everything was taken care of in the event anything happened to him. Obviously that was very much on his mind, given the kind of work he did, both before and after," Fairfax finished, fumbling a bit as he referenced both the CIA work they'd never known of, and the firefighting which had ultimately taken his life.

"Jesus Christ," Cisco said, "is that it? Are you finished? Because from the sound of things, the five of us need to find a place to live."

But the second Cisco said it, they all looked at each other.

They weren't even related to each other.

They were a family in name only, and even that name

hadn't been real. Their father had given all of them a fake name, courtesy of the CIA, but still—

Damn Dad, you could have given us a heads up on this amazing life story you had.

But of course Sonny couldn't have. And now, Nick Marshall was taking over the place they'd always thought was home.

And suddenly Santana realized, though the fog of shock, grief, and yes, even a little fear, that he had nothing, absolutely nothing, to offer Emma Glass.

He wasn't the man he'd thought he was just an hour ago.

Santana Dark wasn't real, not in any way, shape, or form. Neither were the rest of them.

Which meant from this moment on, they were almost reborn—whether they liked it or not.

• • •

Nick Marshall left as soon as he could, without doing more than nodding in the Dark family's direction, and receiving five glares from the other end of the table. He couldn't blame them. Their whole lives had just been ripped apart.

Not only that, but to learn that your father had owed every last penny, every last stick of furniture, to a brother they'd never heard of, had to have been the ultimate insult to the memory of their father.

And since his father had passed away, he was the sole heir.

He got into his black Range Rover, locked the doors, slumped into the seat.

Jesus, what an awful day. It was the last thing he'd expected when he'd come here today. The attorney had been vague when he'd summoned him, telling him that there were estate details that needed to be settled.

He'd thought the attorney had meant his own father's vast estate. Thanks to Nicholas Marshall's business instinct, the Marshall estate was large. Marshall Industries, Inc., owned office buildings and real estate in several states, and some in various locations around the world. He had a helicopter and two jets at his disposal around the clock. A driver was part of his staff, although Nick did much of his own driving. There were "help managers" on every property the Marshall empire owned, just to keep the properties in top shape.

Those people he'd just left—the four brothers and the silver-haired girl—were now homeless because of him.

And it was just the kind of thing Nicholas Marshall III would have done, taking advantage of a brother who was down on his luck, to make a deal, acquire a new property.

Nick could just hear his father. He wouldn't loan or give anybody a dime, so letting his brother have some shred of dignity at death wasn't Nicholas's style. Santiago Quinto Marshall—Sonny Dark—had needed money, and Nicholas had purchased his brother's freedom from debt.

It was all business. His brother's unfortunate life decisions had not been his. That's what Nicholas would say.

In fact, Nicholas would have felt that he'd been plenty charitable allowing the family to stay on the ranch until the day Sonny died. Now it was just a matter of disposing of the ranch and its contents, which Nick Marshall now owned.

He didn't know the first thing about a ranch. He'd grown up living between Dallas, New York City, and Los Angeles. They had home bases in those three cities that were mainly for comfort, and some tax avoidance.

He'd felt Sierra's accusing gaze on him, and felt terrible. Empty somehow. He couldn't blame her for being angry and upset. Devastated, as anyone would be in similar circumstances.

He couldn't even offer to let them stay longer to get their affairs settled, because he already owned the house. According to his father's wishes, he could move in and keep it, similar to the arrangement they had with the three home bases they already owned. Outfit it with staff, etc.

If he didn't want it, the ranch would be liquidated within a year of his father's passing. The brothers had died within two months of each other, but Sonny had passed first. Nicholas would have known of his brother's horrific passing, and yet he hadn't said a word to Nick.

Now, Nick stood to gain a lot of money.

I already have more money than I could ever spend.

His father had set this up so it was all very simple. Cut-and-dry for Nick.

He couldn't imagine ever wanting to live this far from a big city. Had no desire for ranch life. Didn't even have any curiosity about it. Frankly, it wouldn't make sense—too far from the epicenters of big business.

A lake house or beach house, some kind of vacation property, might have made sense. But a working ranch—no.

Strangely enough, he was very curious to see where the beautiful blonde called home. She'd disliked him on the spot, and he couldn't blame her—but he wished he'd met her under far different circumstances. She was just about the most petite, big-eyed thing he'd ever seen.

Nick thought he'd forever be haunted by the pain in those big eyes.

CHAPTER FOUR

The family hunkered down in the living room. Cisco slumped on the leather sofa, and Luke stoked a fire in the massive stone fireplace, though Santana wasn't sure his mind was on the task. Romero poured whiskey into glasses. Santana stood next to Sierra at the window, looking out over the vast Dark property. Cattle moved in the distance, but Santana was more worried about his usually noisy, effervescent sister.

"Do we have any legal recourse?" she asked suddenly, turning from the window.

"Dad had the estate trust air-tight. That's why an irrevocable trust was set up, so that he could meet Nicholas Marshall's terms. A trust makes certain that the estate is disposed of the way the individual wants, in this case, Uncle Nicholas. Our own St. Nick, who rescued our father from debt and cleaned up his mess." Romero handed each of them a glass. "Basically, we're screwed."

"We're not screwed," Sierra said angrily. "I don't care

what those idiot lawyers said. We are still a family. And we're sticking together."

Santana nodded. "I agree with Sierra. We'll go somewhere else. Together. Whatever Pop's problems were, they're not ours."

"Except we don't have a roof over our heads," Luke said.

"It's just a roof," Santana said. "There's millions of roofs in the world. We'll find another."

Cisco turned from beating the firewood into submission with the cast-iron poker. "He's right. There's no reason for us to leave Star Canyon. This is our home."

"I think I'm going," Luke said, his voice soft.

They stared at Luke.

"Going where?" Sierra demanded.

Luke glanced around the house, almost as if he no longer wanted to be in this room. "Think I'll hit the road."

Santana's heart sank. "Let's not make decisions tonight. We're all still in shock."

That was an understatement. He ought to be able to offer comfort and an alternate plan of action to his family.

All he felt was empty.

"I can't believe Dad never told us," Romero said. "He never let on."

"He was of upstanding character our whole lives, at least as we knew him," Luke said. "That's what I'm struggling with the most. In the end, Dad was a liar and maybe worse, to hear the attorneys tell it."

Sierra gasped. "Don't talk about Dad like that! You don't know! Lawyers can be very slimy with the truth."

Santana shrugged. "Let's not let anyone steal the memories of the happy home life we had growing up.

Dad loved us, Mom loved us. He worked hard to keep us together. Let's not let that be destroyed on this new path we find ourselves on."

"Agreed," Sierra said. "We can't let him beat us. He's not going to win."

"Who?" Santana demanded.

"That weasel Marshall." She plopped down in front of the fire, crossing her legs, holding her glass. "I've never met a bigger weasel."

Santana didn't know about weasel, but Nick was as different from them as night was from day.

"He seemed pretty freaked out," Cisco said.

"I don't care about him. He didn't argue that he shouldn't have what was ours," Sierra said. "I hate Nick Marshall and his stupid Marshall Industries, Inc. Isn't that what the attorney said his father did? Owned some big-ass company, which is why Dad knew his brother could help him out?"

"Nick didn't argue," Romero said, "because he owned every bit of this the moment Dad died. That's how irrevocable living trusts work. The estate moves on to the person who is designated executor, and that executor must adhere to the terms of the estate trust. In our case, everything goes to him, by prior arrangement with Dad's brother. In fairness, we've been living on his dime during the time it took the estate to be worked through by the attorneys. I suppose we should have thanked him."

"Bullshit," Sierra muttered, and Luke poured more whiskey into her glass.

"It's so strange we never knew we had an uncle," Luke said. "Dad didn't mention it. As far as we knew, it was just Mom and Dad, and us."

"I get the sense the brothers didn't get along, but I don't know why I feel that way." Santana gulped his whiskey, taking a deep breath. "It must have been hard as hell for Dad to admit he screwed up and go to his brother for a bailout."

"I think Dad got taken advantage of." Sierra wiped her eyes, and Romero handed her a tissue. "Surely his debts weren't so high that he had to sign away everything. It's all that CIA bullshit, and Marshall probably knew he had Dad beat. I feel sorry for Dad."

Santana shook his head. "It doesn't matter now. What we have to focus on is what we're going to do."

"We're going to stick together," Sierra said, "and that means you, too, Luke. No one is going to tear us apart. We're a family, no matter what."

They sat silently, considering the new world they found themselves inhabiting. Sierra was right: they had to stick together, no matter what the future held.

"I can start looking for a place tomorrow," Santana said. "It won't be big, and it won't have land. We'll have to rent, I would imagine, because none of us have the credit or funding to buy a house."

"Unbelievable," Cisco said. "But I'm twenty-five, healthy, and strong. I can join the military, learn a trade, see the world. Some of it, anyway."

Luke nodded. "I'll join you. They'll be happy to take a twenty-three-year-old."

Sierra gasped. "I'm twenty-two."

They all looked at her.

"Yes, you are," Santana said, nodding. "I'm twenty-nine, and Romero's twenty-seven. We'll all young enough to get over this, start over, build again. If Dad could do it with all the challenges he had, we can, too. We'll support each other."

Sierra looked hopeful. "Maybe we have parents somewhere who might want to—"

"No," Santana told his sister gently. "Most likely not. If they'd wanted us to know, they would have found us. Or Dad would have told us." He brushed his sister's long hair over her shoulder and put her head against his chest. "Enough has been stirred up already. I vote we move forward."

"Seconded," Luke said. "I don't really care to find someone who gave me up in the first place."

"That's harsh," Sierra said. "We don't know the circumstances."

"Sorry," Luke said, a touch of bitterness in his tone. "I just don't care about anyone outside of this room."

They sat quietly in front of the fire, lost in their thoughts. It wasn't going to be easy, Santana knew—but they'd get through it.

Their father had left them a legacy, which included independence. Strength. And love.

It was enough.

• • •

There were three weeks until Christmas, the days marching swiftly toward the holidays. Star Canyon was in a festive mood. Pets who came in to see Emma wore cheerful bandanas with candy canes or trees on them. But Emma hadn't seen Santana again. She'd heard about him only through the Star Canyon grapevine.

The grapevine had been humming.

Mary Chapman handed her two bags of leftover scraps for Gus and Bean. "There's no reason to let these go to waste. It's just some bones and a few bits of leftover things that your new babies might like."

Emma smiled. "Thank you. They'll appreciate it."

"There might be some extra in case you have any new strays come in," Mary said.

It happened often enough that Star Canyon stayed on the lookout for animals that had been dumped by uncaring owners. And what was in the bag wouldn't be scraps so much as Mary's weekly offering of chicken and other meats to try to lessen the burden on Emma's clinic. "You have a generous heart, Mary Chapman."

"And you do a good deed by helping out unlucky pets. Now, how about you?"

Emma glanced at the menu. "I'm starved. How about your cucumber sandwich and fruit plate?"

Mary smiled, her eyes bright and cheerful as always. "I guess you've heard the Darks moved out of their house."

Emma stared at Mary, whose expression had, for once, turned quite serious. "I didn't know."

"Apparently Sonny left everything to a brother nobody here ever knew about. The estate was settled last week, and now some out-of-towner owns it all."

Emma froze, stunned, her heart breaking for the Dark family. Mary's worried eyes reflected her own inner sympathy. "I can't believe it."

Mary sat down, straightening her blue shirtwaist dress with a sigh. "It's tragic. And I've heard that Luke and Cisco might enlist. Maybe Romero, too. Obviously everything has changed for them."

"What about the fire department?"

"We'll be short-handed in Star Canyon, but that's the way things go. They have to earn a living now. A small-town fire department can't pay them what they'd need to have homes of their own. Of course, they weren't paying anything for their living situation before."

"Why would Sonny do such a thing?" Emma asked.

"Rumor has it he had made poor financial decisions and had no choice. He'd always focused his kids on community service and taking care of Star Canyon. But we're a poor town, really. Artists like to live here because it's inexpensive. Obviously, the Darks will have to find another way to survive."

"I don't know what to say."

"No one does. No one had a clue Sonny was in trouble."

"What is Santana planning to do?" Emma's heart practically stood still. The last thing she wanted to hear Mary say was that Santana would go back into the military—but it made sense that he would.

"Santana found a house to lease. Captain Martin had a small place outside of town." She got up to greet some customers, came back a moment later with two glasses of tea for them. "The Captain has a few rental properties, so he offered one to the Darks."

The captain of the fire department, Phil Martin, and his wife, Honey, lived in separate houses, and they had for years. No one ever spoke of their odd living arrangement because both Honey and Phil were loved in the town. Honey worked across the street at the small Star Canyon library. Phil kept a few head of cattle, but made extra income by keeping up old houses and renting them out. "It was nice of Phil to help them."

Mary was always happy to talk—discreetly—about the Captain. "Anyway, it's a place for them to start over. They've been moving their clothes out. That's all they have. Furniture, dishes, everything else, stays with the ranch."

"You mean they literally have to leave every single thing behind?"

"Personal items and clothes go with them. Everything else was needed to pay back the debts."

Emma shook her head. The Darks had always been very generous with their time in Star Canyon. It seemed too cruel that along with suffering the death of their beloved father, they should be homeless.

"They'll rebuild," Mary said. "They're strong, tough. True Star Canyon tough." She put a hand on Emma's briefly. "Anyway, he'll be by to see you once he gets things settled, I'm sure."

Emma felt herself blush. "Mary—"

"I know how you feel about that big bear of a man. Your secret's safe with me. I'll get you those cucumber sandwiches now. And you're going to love the fruit I got from the roadside vendors. Beautiful."

She went off, back to being her happy self. Emma didn't think Mary had many bad days—even if the love of her life, Captain Martin, would never be hers.

Emma glanced at her watch. She really needed to get back to the clinic; her lunch hour was half gone. But she was dying to find Sierra. They were close to being the same size, in case she needed to borrow any clothes. And Emma had some extra furniture that was too girly for the men, but might suit Sierra until she got back on her feet.

She'd forgotten to ask where the Darks were renting

their new place. She knew where a few of Phil's properties were, and none were far. It would be easy to get furniture over there if she borrowed a truck.

But thinking about furniture didn't keep her mind off of Santana and his family.

As if she'd conjured them, Sierra and Santana walked in, heading straight to her table when they saw her.

"Can we join you?" Sierra asked, sliding in instantly when Emma nodded.

Santana didn't quite meet her gaze the way he had before. She sensed a new reserve in his manner, and her heart cracked a little.

"I'm sure you've heard things have been a little crazy around our place." Sierra smiled, determined to be positive about everything. "We have a new home."

"I just heard." Across the table, Santana's demeanor was foreboding and maybe a little aloof. "I'm so sorry," she said, barreling ahead with her true feelings.

"It's all right. We'll be fine. It was just a shock, that's all." Sierra took a deep breath. "What are you eating?"

"Cucumber sandwiches," Emma said miserably. "What can I do to help you guys?"

Mary came over to the table with two glasses of tea. "Hello, friends and neighbors."

"Hi, Mary," Sierra said. "What's good today?"

"Whatever you want is on the house," Mary said.

"We don't need anything on the house," Santana said. "We can pay, Mary."

Mary's face fell.

"Santana!" Sierra socked her brother in the arm. "I'm so sorry, Mary! My brother must be suffering from asshole-itis today!" She patted Mary's arm. "We'll have cucumber sandwiches like Emma." Sierra glanced at her brother. "Maybe throw a little chicken on my brother's sandwich. I think he's suffering from hunger or something that brought out the rude in him."

"No problem," Mary murmured, hurrying off.

Emma averted her gaze, swamped in misery.

"I think I'll get going," Santana said.

"No, you won't." Sierra glared at her brother. "You'll sit here and not insult any more of our lifelong friends."

To Emma's surprise, Santana sighed and did exactly as his sister demanded.

"We're not in our best place, mentally," Sierra said. "Forgive us."

Santana looked at Emma. "How are the boys?"

"Growing too fast. We're working on basic commands, now that they've settled in a bit." She looked at Sierra, not able to meet Santana's gaze any longer. "If you want a job, I always need help at the vet clinic."

Sierra looked up. "Me? Oh, no, thank you. That's so sweet of you." She beamed. "I'm thinking about opening a bridal shop."

Santana groaned. "We don't need fairy tales right now, Sierra. We need cold, hard reality."

"I'm done with reality." She took a deep breath. "We don't talk about it, but it destroyed us when Dad died. And maybe it was harder on you than the rest of us because you couldn't be here for his memorial. You weren't here the night Captain Martin came to tell us what happened."

Emma wished she were anywhere but here during this

private family moment. She could hear the shattered anguish in Sierra's voice; nothing had ever torn Emma so much.

"Santana, we lost our home, and those asshole lawyers say we're not a family. That Dad was some sort of operative who lived a high-risk lifestyle and developed problems later." She shook her head. "I'm done with that reality. I'm either opening a bridal shop and spending my time around happy people, or I'm joining the fire department." She pinned her brother with a steely gaze. "Frankly, I'm more suited to the fire department, but I think it would kill you if I did it."

"No," Santana said quietly. "No fires."

"Then support me," Sierra said. "You're not the only lost soul around here."

Emma glanced at Santana, surprised to find his gaze on her. She tried to smile, freezing when Sierra suddenly gasped. "What's our worst nightmare doing here?"

Emma whipped around to see what a worst nightmare looked like. For one thing, he was really handsome. They weren't the only ones gawking—strangers came through Star Canyon to visit the artists' galleries, and for the occasional stroll through a town that time seemed to have forgotten—but they didn't look like this man.

He was strong and tall. His hair was cut in a classic style, the brown-and-gold sun streaks natural from being outdoors. He looked like he spent a lot of time outside, though his suit said otherwise.

"What's he doing here?" Sierra demanded again, her tone bitter.

"Coming to see his new house. Remember, he either has to take it over or sell it." Santana rose. "If you can't beat them, join them, right?"

"What are you doing?" Sierra hissed at her brother, but it was too late. Santana walked over to the newcomer, greeting him, if not warmly.

Emma was astonished when he brought the man to their table.

"Have a seat," Santana said. "This is my sister, Sierra."

"I remember." He nodded, saying nothing else.

Sierra glared at him.

"And this is Emma Glass, our resident vet. Emma, this is Nick Marshall."

Emma didn't know what to do other than put out her hand for him to shake.

"Nice to make your acquaintance, Emma." He didn't let the lack of warmth from her or her friend daunt him as he took the seat next to Emma.

Never had a booth felt so small. Emma glanced at Sierra, distressed, but her friend's gaze was locked on Nick, with no apparent need to hide her feelings.

"This is awkward as hell," Nick said.

"We're going to have to work around it." Santana waved Mary over, and Mary came running with a menu, eager to be included. "Mary, this is Nick Marshall. He's come out to see our old place."

"Welcome to Star Canyon, Nick," Mary said, apparently the only one of them with any real manners, Emma thought.

Nick glanced at Sierra, who was most decidedly not friendly. "Thank you."

"What can I get you?"

"Ah—" Nick began, and Emma thought he really didn't want to eat with them.

"You might like a chicken sandwich on fresh-baked bread," Mary suggested.

Nick shot a careful look at Santana's plate. "Coffee, please. Black."

Mary looked distressed, and maybe a little embarrassed. Aware that he might look like he was too good for the locals, Nick cleared his throat. "If you wouldn't mind, I'll have some of those cucumber sandwiches everyone else is having."

Everyone stared at him, but Nick seemed oblivious. "My mother made cucumber sandwiches," he said with a smile meant to put Mary at ease. "I haven't had one in many years, and those look delicious."

Sunshine parting clouds couldn't have looked brighter than the smile on Mary's face. She hurried off to get Nick's order.

Santana cleared his throat. "We're not always socially awkward."

"Yes, we are," Sierra said, determined. "This is a small town. We do awkward very well."

Nick smiled at Emma. "So, a vet."

She nodded. "Yes. I took over my father's practice last year." She couldn't have said why she was suddenly determined to make him feel more comfortable, except that everyone at the table was behaving like they were completely different people than they normally were. "You'll call me for any problems you might have with your cattle."

That fell on the table like a stack of wet newspapers no one wanted.

"Big and small animal vet?" Nick asked curiously, not seeming to notice the pointed disregard coming from Sierra.

"Yes. Until someone comes along that wants to join my practice and take one side or the other, I'm doing both."

"I'm not going to keep the cattle," Nick said, and Sierra stiffened. "Or the horses, I imagine."

Sierra got up. "I'm going. Santana, you can get a ride from Nick. He won't mind taking you to our old home, I'm sure."

She went off, a blur of tight jeans and a rose-printed western shirt that for some reason seemed to catch Nick's eye. Probably didn't see too many real, honest-to-goodness cowgirls wherever it was that he came from. "I'm going to go with your sister," Emma said, hopping up so the two men could talk. "Nice meeting you, Nick." She hurried out after Sierra.

"Sierra, wait! I'll drive you." Emma caught up to her friend.

"No, thanks. I just want to…I don't know. Get away from this town for a while. Maybe forever." She got into her truck and drove away. Emma stared after her, feeling sad for her, for the whole Dark family.

"You left this," she heard behind her, and whirled to find Santana staring down at her. He handed over the doggie bag Mary was donating to her new puppies. "Gus and Bean would appreciate it if you don't leave it behind."

"Thank you," Emma said, breathless suddenly in the cold bursts of icy breeze blowing up under her collar. "I'm so sorry about everything."

"I know. So am I."

He tipped his hat and went back inside. Emma stared after him, realizing with a sinking heart that the old Santana she'd waited so long for him to return home had changed overnight. Changed into someone who clearly wanted to forget about their kiss, and the closeness that had been developing between them since he'd come back to Star Canyon.

Without him saying a word, she could tell it was over before it had even gotten started.

Which broke her heart, that heart that had waited almost half her life for him to realize that he was the only man she could ever truly love.

. . .

Santana took a second to eyeball Nick before he returned to his seat. He had to give the man credit; he didn't look as uncomfortable as he had to feel.

Then again, commercial real estate was the kingdom Nick's father—Santana's mysterious uncle-in-name-only—had built. A ranch was probably nothing to him. Just business as usual.

"Sorry about that. I didn't tell my sister you were coming out." He sighed. "I was going to, but I got sidetracked." He'd chickened out, he realized, and Sierra had paid the price. And Nick.

"No problem. I understand." Nick sipped his coffee, and Santana had to work really hard to remember that he wasn't supposed to like this guy. There was no reason to like him. They were on opposite sides of a very messed up situation. But Nick seemed determined to let all the bad vibes wash right over him.

"She doesn't know I called you. But I think it's best if I walk you through some things, since you're—"

"New to town," Nick finished, when Santana had been unable to say *the new owner of our ranch.* "I get it. I appreciate you meeting me."

They finished their food, and Santana waited for the check. Mary's cheeks turned a bit pink as she handed him the slip.

"I'm sorry as hell about my mouth earlier, Mary," he said.

"Don't think another thing of it," Mary said quickly.

Nick handed her a credit card. "I'm buying. It's the least I can do."

"That's not necessary—" Santana began.

Mary grabbed the card. "What a courteous thing to do," she said, hurrying off with his plastic.

Santana drummed his fingers on the table, unable to look at the man he'd invited to town. He thought about Emma again, and how stunned she'd looked by the new turn of events.

"You didn't have to move out so quickly," Nick said. "According to the trust, you had another six months."

"It was better this way." He rose, thinking ties to the past were sometimes better cut quickly and efficiently. "Come on. I'll show you around."

. . .

Emma was surprised when Santana showed up at the clinic just as she was leaving. "Hi," she said, acting as if her heart hadn't just started beating weirdly.

"Thought I might take you to dinner. If you're available." He cleared his throat. "I'd sure like to."

She swallowed, not certain why he was asking. He'd been so distant today at lunch. "Any particular reason?"

"Sierra asked me to," he said, and right then, Emma knew this wasn't a romantic dinner request.

What was new about that? "I have to pass. Thanks, though. I've got to exercise the dogs, feed the cat, tend the glass menagerie." She stopped, blushing. "God, that sounds nerdy. I really didn't mean to say that."

He smiled, for the first time since she'd seen him that day. "Come out with me. Sierra will chew my ear off if you don't."

"Make a girl feel good, why don't you?" She hopped in his truck when he unlocked the passenger side door. "So you're going to help me walk animals, give me a chance to shower, and then take me to dinner because your sister asked you to? It's a lot of work for a simple dinner."

"Yeah, well. Sierra says I owe you a meal because I was such a jerk at lunch."

She pulled down the visor so she could look at herself, winding her hair up a bit tighter into its typical ponytail. "I didn't think you were a jerk. Things have changed in your life, and I understand. Anyway, I'm used to you being sort of out of reach."

He took the road toward her house. "Out of reach?"

"Yeah. You were the guy all the girls had a crush on in high school. But apparently you rarely dated unless there was some kind of dance coming up."

"I was not the town's most sought-after bachelor, but thanks for trying to sell me that way. My ego likes it, even if it's not true."

He was very sought-after then, and no doubt now, as all

the Dark men had been. For that matter, the local boys had loved Sierra—not that Sierra had been more than friends with any of them. "So what's so important that Sierra can't ask me herself?"

"My sister hasn't been herself since—since we found out everything."

"I can imagine," Emma murmured.

"So now she's decided to open this wedding shop."

"Sounds like a lovely idea."

"Except we don't have any weddings to speak of in Star Canyon."

Emma looked out the window. "Sierra didn't ask you to take me out, did she? You want me to help you with your sister."

"There's a reason you were our class valedictorian."

He pulled into the drive leading to her small, white gingerbread-style Victorian home. "So what is it?"

"I'm hoping you'll talk to her."

They got out of the truck. Emma carried the bag of dog treats to the door, unlocked it. "Be prepared for the howling horde. They're all going to want their supper and some attention."

Gus and Bean were ecstatic to see Santana, the blue Persian less enthusiastic. Emma fed the lovebirds while Gus and Bean raced outside with Santana, and as she peeped out the window, she could see that no walk would be needed immediately. He'd dug a ball out of his truck, probably one of Joe's, and was throwing it for Gus and Bean. To her astonishment, the dogs loved running after it, and would bring it back to Santana to do again. They weren't perfect, they didn't drop the ball right at his boots, but they loved racing each other to get the tennis ball first.

That gave her time to quickly change the cat litter and hop in the shower. It had been a long day at the clinic, with a couple of involved surgeries, and a shower was just what she needed to get ready to tell Santana that Sierra was going to do whatever she wanted to, regardless of anything anyone said to her.

Surely he knew that. He had to. She sensed more than anything, he was worried about his little sister. Maybe just talking about it would ease his mind.

She grabbed a soft blue cashmere dress that tied at her waist, a pair of brown cowboy boots, fluffed her hair, put on lipstick and a little mascara, made sure she spritzed herself with perfume.

She looked like she was trying to catch a sexy SEAL.

Maybe she was.

• • •

Santana swallowed hard when Emma walked out of her bedroom. He'd made sure the dogs had fresh water for their lolling tongues, and they panted heavily, sort of like he felt at the moment he laid eyes on Emma's curves in the blue dress. He'd always known she was sexy, but sexy-in-a-blue-dress was more than he'd been prepared for.

"You look…very nice."

She smiled. "Thanks."

"Shall we go?" he suddenly asked. "I think I've worn the boys out for the moment."

"Sure." She grabbed her purse. "I warn you, this dinner won't turn out the way you're hoping."

He felt the back of his neck turn a bit warm. Damn, she'd read his mind, picked up on the lust calling him. Or maybe he was staring like a hungry…like Gus and Bean after the tennis ball, all bug-eyed and eager. "I'm not sure I'm hoping for anything," he said, telling one of the biggest fibs of his entire day.

"No one can help you with Sierra. You know your sister's going to do whatever she wants."

Oh, jeez. He told his heart to stop hammering. "So, Jenny's not babysitting the boys anymore?"

They walked outside, and Emma locked up. "She usually checks on them throughout the day if she can't stay with them. They're still too young and a little skittish to be left all day. When she can't come over, I try to come home at lunch. I couldn't today, though."

"It was good of you to sit with us. Sorry it was so uncomfortable." He started the truck.

"Not for me." He felt her gaze on him. "I'm so sorry for what you're going through."

"It's getting better every day." He wasn't being truthful. He was damn worried about Sierra, as were his brothers. Of course, he was worried about them, too. The stress and grief were taking their toll on his family in different ways. "Fuck it. It's not getting better at all. But you've been a good friend to our family, Emma."

He didn't know how to put into words the problem that had unexpectedly exploded their world. All he knew was that he couldn't offer Emma anything. And she sat there, all sexy as hell in her blue dress, her big eyes drinking him in.

And all he wanted to be able to say was how crazy he was about her, how much he wanted to taste her lips again, feel her in his arms.

"I wish I was at a different place in life," he said instead.

"What do you mean?"

"Everything changed," he said quietly. "Nothing is ever going to be the same."

CHAPTER FIVE

Nick Marshall was the world's biggest douche, and if he didn't stay the hell away from her family, Sierra planned to tell him in words that even a giant Poindexter douche like him could understand. Just because he'd landed a huge inheritance thanks to the real estate finesse of their father, didn't mean what he'd done was fair or right. She'd found out by looking through extensive old records of their father's how much money Sonny had owed his brother, and it hadn't been any five million dollars.

Closer to one million—not that anybody seemed to be counting their supposed millions.

And yet somehow, the entire amount, every stick of their furniture, every head of cattle, went to that suit wearing frat daddy. And he wasn't going to say a word about the unfairness of the whole thing. Didn't apologize for his father taking advantage of his brother, whom he had to have known needed help. Being in a witness protection program couldn't have been easy. There'd been seven mouths to feed as well. And she'd looked up Marshall Industries, Inc., astonished by the company's holdings. Then she'd found one of Nick's houses, feeling no guilt at all when she pulled up the image.

The thing was a fricking castle. And that was just one of his "homes."

So here he was, a vulture, picking over the bones of the Darks. Not troubled at all by his father's predatory instincts and lifestyle, nor that his living family relations—distant, of course, hanging by an in-name-only thread—would lose their only roof, while he had several roofs.

How dare he show up like he belonged in this town?

"Sierra!"

She jumped at her brother's bellow. "What?"

"Could you join us, please?"

Reluctantly, she went out, faced Nick and Santana, and Emma. Nick was lucky she didn't give him a swift kick to the shin or a piece of her mind, whichever felt better. "You roared, brother?"

"I should be going," Emma said.

"Stay," Sierra said. "Mr. Marshall won't be here long."

It finally seemed to hit him that they weren't serfs on his lordship's estate. "I've been looking around the property, and there's a lot of work that needs to be done."

"No kidding," Sierra said. "You're really smart. Probably have a Harvard diploma and everything, don't you?"

He looked slightly uncomfortable. "Actually, yes."

She wanted to slap him right then, but what would it serve? She was happy to see she'd at least seemed to get it through his thick skull that he was a privileged prick.

Nick cleared his throat, clearly at a loss and groping for

words. "There are five of you, and one of me, and as I don't know the first thing about this type of property—"

"Let me stop you right there." If Sierra had one wish, it was that the man wasn't so devastatingly handsome. But she couldn't allow that to sidetrack her. "You want our help."

"There's a lot to do." Nick nodded. "Yes, I'd like to hire Santana to run the place."

"As a foreman?" Santana asked.

"That's a bit wrong," Sierra said. "Do you have any idea what you're asking, you pinhead suit?"

Nick blinked, obviously never being exposed to anyone who called him what he was. "Actually, I do, and I've discussed it with the attorneys, and they said that there's nothing that violates the terms of the estate trust if I hire Santana to run the ranch."

Emma had gone back outside. Sierra was embarrassed of this shack, and pissed at Nick, so she shrugged. "Discuss it with my brother." She left to find Emma.

"This sucks," she said to Emma when she found her standing on the worn concrete drive. "What a freak. I don't even think he knows he's a freak."

Emma stifled a giggle, and Sierra grinned. "Well, he is."

Nick came outside. "I don't suppose you'd allow me to buy dinner for you, so we could discuss this?"

In that split second, Sierra realized an unfortunate fact about the freakish Nick Marshall: in spite of his money and good looks, despite having everything plus the gold spoon and no doubt the golden platter that went with it, rich whiz kid Nick Marshall was lonely.

Santana glanced her way, shrugging, clearly signaling that it was up to her.

"You already bought our lunch," she said.

"Still, I'm trying to get assistance from you."

He gave her a winning smile that probably sank women's hearts and earned him seats on company boards or something. He'd learn quickly that Star Canyon wasn't a country club to wheel and deal in. "Whatever," she said coldly.

• • •

"Sierra!" Emma exclaimed when Nick returned inside, looking a bit deflated. "What has gotten into you?"

"Nothing at all."

Emma stopped, pulling Sierra to a stop. "You haven't been yourself all day. Apparently not for a while, either, because your brother is worried about you."

"He shouldn't be. I'm fine. It's everybody around me who is having issues."

Emma wasn't so sure. "Then go back in there and give Santana a chance to decide if he wants a job."

"A job?" Sierra pulled her black knit scarf up higher on her neck. "Why would Santana want to work for that ass?"

"Because it's a job, and jobs are hard to find in Star Canyon."

"I'm not stopping Santana from taking a job. Anyone in town would hire my brother."

"No, but he won't take the job with Nick, if he thinks it will make you unhappy. Think about it, Sierra. Your brother is just back from being deployed. You guys are living in a rental house. I'm positive Santana would like to at least think about an offer of work at the ranch." Talking sense into Sierra at this moment was a task not to be undertaken lightly. "He said he'd planned to work there when it was still the Dark—"

"I just don't like him."

"No one says you have to marry him. I'm going to go tell the guys we're waiting on them. And for the record, peacemaker isn't a role I exactly covet. You guys are going to have to take pity on me. I'm a veterinarian. I specialize in canine and feline emotions, not necessarily human ones."

Sierra snorted as Emma jogged up the wooden steps and let the front door of the house announce her presence with a slight slam. The men turned to look at her.

"Sierra has decided a burger in Lightning Canyon sounds delicious," Emma announced.

"How did you talk her into that?" Nick asked.

"First lesson from your new foreman," Santana said, "never ask too many questions."

"I like it." Nick opened the door, and Santana held it for her so she could walk out.

"Thanks," Santana told her. "It's not easy to bring Sierra around."

"No problem. It wasn't hard to change her mind." She glanced over his broad shoulders, found herself caught by his deep eyes for just a split second, then hurried to the truck.

The truth was, she wanted to have dinner with him tonight. Maybe friends was the best they could be right now, but wasn't that better than nothing?

CHAPTER SIX

It was on the drive to Lightning Canyon that Santana realized Emma and Sierra weren't themselves. The two of them sat silent in the back seat of the Ranger Rover, which was strange for both of them. Nick made pleasant conversation, when he was the one who should be feeling out of place.

Emma mostly stared outside the car window. Sierra fell asleep, her head lolling.

"This is it," Santana announced, and Nick parked at Lightning Canyon's best spot for burgers. Sierra pulled herself to an upright position, blinking owlishly around, scowling at Nick.

It was very clear Sierra imitated the seating chart at lunch. She squeezed in next to Emma before Santana had a chance to get in the booth next to her. Sierra glared at Nick, and took her menu from the waitress, opening it with a disgruntled flourish.

Emma hid a smile, and Santana thought it was big of Nick to ignore the darts being thrown at him.

"Shall we start with a bottle of wine?" Nick asked.

Santana winced. "It's BYOB here, actually. Bring your own bottle, and in this town, that means beer or wine, nothing harder."

"Ah." Nick nodded, looking slightly surprised but clearly trying to roll with it. "Where do we get a bottle of good wine, then?"

"You have to cross some palms with silver," Santana said, and Emma glanced at him.

"There's no choice wine in this town," Sierra told Nick pointedly. "Do you always sound like you should be sitting in an upper-crust country club?"

"Do I?" Nick asked. "I wasn't aware wine was a social marker."

Sierra rolled her eyes. "I would have respected you maybe a little if you weren't trying to pair wine with a burger."

"Sierra," Santana said, "discreetly speak to Señor Hernandez, will you?"

"Let me provide the silver," Nick said, pulling out his wallet. "This is my treat." He cleared his throat, and Santana felt slightly sorry for him. The man was so far out of his depth he probably didn't even realize it.

"How much silver is required for whatever adult beverage might be served in this establishment?" Nick asked.

They all stared at Nick's leather passport wallet. Santana carried his money wrapped around his credit cards with a rubber band, as his father had, as did most men in the town, regardless of their financial well being.

"We can handle the silver," Santana said, reaching into his pocket. He handed Sierra a couple of tens. "Thanks, Sierra."

Nick watched Sierra leave and walk across the street. Emma noticed Nick's interested gaze, too.

Emma looked at her menu. Nick studied the TVs in the upper aeries of the café, and watched the line dancers in the back, shuffling across the floor in boots. Sierra came back in with a six-pack of Dos she set on the table.

"*Señor* says to tell you *hola*. And that he's glad you're back." Sierra beamed. "He says the Dos is on him to celebrate your safe return."

"Safe return from where?" Nick asked, and Santana shook his head.

Emma lost her focus on the menu. "Santana's just back from being deployed."

Nick's gaze returned to him. "Deployed?"

"Got back a few weeks ago. I was in the Middle East," he said slowly, realizing that for the first time, he wasn't feeling anxiety about retiring from the Navy. He didn't feel bottled up; he didn't feel spent.

He felt just fine, the way he had in the old days, before his father had died, before they'd lost the ranch, before he'd realized that one more tour of duty would be one too many. Tempting the gods wasn't wise. He'd come through four tours in better shape than most.

Of course, the gods had quixotic personalities, and were trying to lure his younger brothers away instead. Maybe they'd follow the rodeo, maybe try out some caves in Belize. Romero hadn't clarified.

Hell, for all he knew, Romero had decided to join Luke and Cisco and give the military life a shot, now that they had no ranch to work.

"Thank you for your service," Nick said, and Santana started.

"No need to thank me." He passed around the beers, wishing he was sitting next to Emma.

"I appreciate your agreeing to take the job as foreman," Nick said.

"Why? Do you get a tax credit for hiring a veteran?" Sierra demanded.

Santana shrugged. "I'm taking the job, and I'm grateful for it, Nick."

When the waitress came over, they all ordered the same thing: Burgers, well-done, veggies on the side. The waitress left, and Nick lifted his bottle. "Thanks, guys."

"Stop being so nice," Sierra snapped. "You got our ranch, you don't need to rub salt in the wound by showing us what a prince you are."

Emma's mouth fell open as she stared at Sierra. Nick looked startled, and Santana shook his head.

"Sierra, Nick had nothing to do with the agreement our fathers brokered. I can work for him and help him make a success of things, or he'll put the ranch on the market and it will be sold, as per the trust, which was an irrevocable trust, remember?" He looked at his sister, unwilling to hurt her, but knowing he had to make her understand. "Very likely Mr. Marshall made his brother agree to an irrevocable trust because he didn't want to leave open the possibility that he might predecease Dad, and Dad might change the will in our favor. Given that Dad had shown that he was capable of making disastrous financial decisions, it was a wise business decision to make it irrevocable. If I don't help Nick, and he can't make it work or decides to sell, some developer is going to come along and pour concrete over our ranch, and change Star Canyon forever. Not to mention, I'm pretty happy to have employment for however long, doing what I know how to do best. What I love doing most of all."

Sierra waited as the waitress set down their plates.

"Everything look all right?" she asked. "I can take your burgers back if they're not how you like them."

"Mine's fine," Nick said with a smile Santana thought seemed very genuine for a man who wasn't used to greasy spoons and roadside cafes.

They all nodded, and when the waitress left, Sierra looked at Nick. "I don't understand why you'd want to live at our ranch. You're not a working ranch kind of man."

He shrugged, unbothered as he picked up his burger. "I need to do it. And since your brother's going to help me out, maybe you'd be interested in working at the ranch, too."

Emma's gaze met Santana's over the open warfare that had been declared at the table. "I'm opening a bridal store, if you most know," Sierra announced.

Nick raised a brow. "How many weddings are there a year in Star Canyon? Based on the town rolls of five hundred people, give or take a dozen depending on the weather and when someone's decided to look for greener pastures, I'd put the number at less than ten."

Sierra leaned back, her gaze cool. "So you've checked out our historic little town."

"A good businessman looks into what he's investing in."

"So we're an investment," Sierra said, and Emma put down her burger.

"Sierra, aren't you hungry?" Emma asked.

"Why did you decide to take over the ranch?" Sierra asked.

"Maybe I'm looking for peace and quiet."

Sierra looked outraged, Santana noted, and outrage on his sister was a bad thing. "Sierra," Santana began, but she sprang to her feet.

"I don't know why I agreed to break bread with the enemy. And you *are* the enemy," she told Nick. "I came to dinner to protect my brother from your sneaky, opportunistic ways, because Santana has a good heart. He doesn't want to believe that you're conniving. But your father was, and I think you are, too." She looked at Santana. "I can't protect you if you decide to jump right into the lion's jaws. But I'd look before you leap. I'm catching a ride back to Star Canyon." She grabbed her purse and looked at Emma. "Sorry, Emma."

"It's fine." Emma snatched her purse up and followed Emma to the door, saying, "Thanks for dinner, Nick," over her shoulder as she hurried after his sister.

Santana stared after the two women as they departed.

"I should offer them a ride home," Nick said. He dug around in his pocket for his wallet. Patted his trousers for his keys.

"Don't worry," Santana said with a sigh, as he realized what had happened. "Sierra is driving home right now in a very nice Ranger Rover. I'll have the waitress go across the street and pick us up some more brew."

Nick stared at him. "Are you saying your sister picked my pocket before we ever got inside the restaurant?"

"It's probably best if we don't discuss the particulars."

Nick leaned back in the booth. "How's her driving?"

"Passable." No sense in telling the man that right now, his Range Rover was probably surpassing any previous record the odometer had ever experienced. The women probably had the windows rolled down, were very likely singing at the top of their lungs all the way back to town.

"So is there a taxi service from here to Star Canyon?" Nick asked.

"There's a service, though I don't know if I'd call it a taxi." Santana lifted his bottle in a mock salute. "Have another beer, cousin. You're going to need it."

• • •

Emma followed Sierra out, not shocked at all that they were stealing a ride home. Sierra wasn't easily intimidated, and she was tough like her brothers, and taking Nick's fancy car for a joy ride would be a distraction for her. Emma decided her best option was to stick with her friend and make sure she stayed out of more trouble.

Once home, Emma sank into the wicker seat on her white-painted porch, Gus and Bean happy to be out in the front yard, despite December's chill. She pulled the blanket a little further around her, enjoying the bright stars in a velvety sky and a half slice of moon pinned among them.

It was probably only thirty minutes later, after she'd gone in to make herself a cup of hot cocoa and returned to her wicker seat, that she heard a truck in her drive. She wasn't totally surprised to see Santana park his truck and amble up to the porch.

"Can't sleep after a meal like that one?" he called, when he couldn't make it farther without Gus and Bean joyously halting him for attention.

"I thought Star Canyon was where all the excitement is, anyway."

"The excitement is where Sierra is. Can I join you?"

"Help yourself."

He sank into the wicker seat beside her. "I tried calling. And texting. Figured I'd better drop by, make sure you were all right." He looked at her. "You rode home with Sierra in a snit, in a car she stole. I was worried."

"Borrowed. We borrowed it."

"Still." He let out a long breath. "I didn't realize my sister was as angry as she is. *Is* as angry as she is. In retrospect, I see her point."

"How did you guys get back to town?" Emma didn't want to discuss their personal family issues.

"By a mode of transportation I can assure you that Nicholas Marshall IV has never traveled before. In the back of Señor Hernandez's truck he uses to haul hay." He chuckled softly, and the sound sizzled along Emma's nerves, surprising her. He was sexy, oh-so-sexy, which she'd always known—but it wasn't just the sexy she found so attractive.

"How did Nick feel about riding in a truck?"

"The truck bed. We rode in the truck bed with the hay bales and a couple of farm hands that didn't speak the world's best English. Nick seemed to enjoy himself thoroughly. Or he has damn good manners and wasn't letting on." He laughed, and the sound was rich and full in the night. She leaned back, comforted by Santana's strength. "Let's just say the experience didn't devastate him the way I would have imagined it might. Getting his white shirt dirty didn't seem to faze him."

"I'm not surprised, actually."

"I have the strangest feeling that Nick and his father might have been cut from two very different pieces of cloth."

Emma watched Gus and Bean wrestling with a smile. The two German shepherd puppies scrabbled playfully, and then all of a sudden, sat up straight, their ears perked toward the bushes.

"They heard their first owl," Emma whispered.

After a minute of watching the dogs try to figure out exactly what was hooting nearby, Santana said, "Do you think I'm nuts to work for Nick?"

"No. It's a great idea. Certainly no nuttier than opening a bridal shop in a town that has, as Nick pointed out, a handful of weddings a year."

"I thought my sister was going to go up in smoke when he said that." Santana chuckled. "I shouldn't laugh, but Nick's clearly done some due diligence on what he's getting himself into in Star Canyon. And Sierra didn't want to hear a word of practical criticism of her new project."

Emma smiled. "Sierra is my dear friend. If she wants to open a bridal shop, I'll support her. I'll even put her business cards in my clinic."

He was silent. Gus and Bean settled at their feet, worn out from playing. "Have I mentioned I'm a little worried about Sierra?"

She didn't want to say it, but she was, too.

"Ever since we found out about everything, she hasn't been herself."

"You've lost the only home you've ever known. You're taking a job with a man your sister refers to as the enemy, and you're just now getting to grieve, Santana." Emma considered her words carefully. "Maybe none of you have been the same ever since your father died. It would be very understandable."

"I think the reason I'm taking the job with Nick is to stay near the old place."

"It won't drive you insane? Working there, but knowing it's no longer your home?" Emma looked at him curiously.

"There's nothing I can do about the past. What happened, happened, and clearly none of us knew Dad the way we thought we did." He leaned back, his shoulder brushing hers in a way that felt companionable. "I figure helping Nick manage the place keeps it in his hands, instead of letting somebody take it over that will chop it up into small lots for homes. I'm being selfish, I suppose."

"I should get everybody to bed," she said softly. "I fall asleep early, in case I get an emergency call in the night. Routine is everything in my business."

He stood when she did.

Oh, she had good intentions. She was trying to convince herself more than Santana. So when he leaned down to kiss her goodnight, Emma closed her eyes, almost relieved when his lips touched hers. Her whole body yearned to be close to his, as if she'd waited forever to be in his arms. She wanted so badly to pull his head closer to hers, get as close to him as she possibly could.

"Wait a minute." She pulled back, looked up at him. "Why are you kissing me?"

He hesitated for a fraction of a second. "Since saying *because I want to* isn't the answer you're looking for…I guess I have to admit that I'm just as intrigued by you as Nick is by my sister." He touched the curve of her cheek. "The only difference is that Nick doesn't know why he's fascinated by Sierra, and he'll probably end up getting third-degree burns. I, on the other hand, know exactly why you fascinate me."

"You said everything had changed," Emma reminded him, "I *know* everything has changed for you. You sounded very clear about having developed a sudden case of cold feet."

"I'm not going to say that I've handled this whole new-cousin-takes-over-the-ranch and you're-all-adopted scenario very well. Probably I haven't handled it one bit." He shrugged and suddenly released her, as if he'd had second thoughts and was fighting temptation. "You're right. There's things I need to work out. You're the one thing in my life that's stayed constant, and I guess I'm drawn to that. Which isn't fair to you. All I know is that when I'm around you, I want you like nothing I've ever wanted. Frankly, I'd give anything to be the man who deserves you, Emma Glass."

He gave the puppies a swift pat on their heads, delighting them, and let himself out.

"And that," she told Gus and Bean, "is how to run a guy off in record time."

Santana had wanted her—she'd felt it, in the way he caressed her face, the way his strong arms held her close. And he'd admitted it, with that husky, gentle tone in his voice, the passion barely disguised as he spoke.

A shiver ran over her.

For just the briefest of seconds, Emma desperately wished she'd been brave enough to ask him to stay—in spite of everything.

But unlike Sierra, she wasn't the kind of woman who took a lot of chances.

She'd never taken a chance on anything, she realized, as she looked around her pretty blue-painted bedroom with the white comforter on the bed, her one frivolous luxury in spite of the pets and her veterinary work. Everything else in her life could be furry, muddy, covered with cat paws—but not her room. This was her sanctuary, her reservoir.

But life in Star Canyon was about taking chances. Half of them didn't work out. Half of them did.

Proceed with caution had always been her motto.

Yet if she'd thrown that motto out tonight, Santana would be in this bed with her right now.

A knock sounded on her door. She opened it, her heart leaping. "Did you forget something?" she asked Santana.

"We need to get your Jeep if you want to get to work in the morning."

She could call Jenny. Jenny would be happy to come by early and give her a ride to the clinic.

Or…

She held the door open. "Or you can drop me off in the morning."

Heat flared in his eyes. She nearly melted on the spot, alive with wanting him. On a limb, waiting for his answer, Emma wondered if she'd done the right thing. Maybe she sounded desperate, considering the conversation they'd just had. It had seemed so final.

All she knew was that she wanted Santana in her arms more than anything in the world.

He drew in a deep breath. For one wild moment, she thought he was going to turn her down flat.

He closed the door, his gaze strange with darkness, and pulled her up against his chest, kissing her with the heat she needed. Had been waiting for forever. She clung to his sheepskin jacket, lost in what he was doing to her mouth. Her soul.

She heard a moan, realized it was her. He pulled her to him even closer, his mouth harder on hers now, searching, tasting. She pulled back. "Santana—"

He ignored her hesitation, pulled her back to him, his mouth demanding on hers. She felt fire start taking her over, melted against him with a moan. His mouth felt so good. He held her so tight, so hard, that she knew he wanted her. And she wanted him, so much she felt like she was falling into an abyss. But he caught her before she fell, his arms strong, his kisses demanding and insistent, making her body awaken from a slumber she hadn't realized had claimed her.

"Take me to bed," she whispered against his mouth.

He stilled with a groan, his mouth angled against hers, then nudged her lips open, sweeping inside her, searching. Didn't he want her? That thought was instantly perished as he crushed her up against her chest, carrying her down the hall to her room.

He tossed back the white comforter with one hand and laid her down. He looked at her, his eyes dark and haunted. She waited, her breath coming in small pants.

"Santana—"

"You're beautiful," he said. "I've dreamed of seeing you like this. Being with you." He pulled off her boots, dropping them to the floor. She moved, thinking to help undress him, but he pressed her back against the pillows. "I just want to look at it, just like this." He picked up her hand, kissed her fingertips. "I've waited years for this moment."

Her heart raced in a mad tattoo. Slowly, he pulled off her socks, removed her jeans with the care that one would reveal a rare piece of art. She watched fire born in his eyes as he met hers, realized there was no going back from this precipice in their relationship. The dogs snuffled at the door, but Santana didn't seem to hear. She lay still, wanting desperately to touch Santana, feel his hard muscles—recognized he was savoring every moment, every motion together. She'd never been the object of a man's desire before—not this kind of intense desire—and it felt like her breath might stop any moment if he didn't touch her. Hold her.

He put his warm palm against her belly, stroked the lace at the top of her black panties, undid the buttons of her blouse one by one, pushing the blouse away from her black bra with a groan. Desperate for him to touch her, and to run her hands over every inch of her body, Emma squirmed. "Santana, don't make me wait."

His gaze met hers. She couldn't stand it another second. Rising to her knees, she tugged off his shirt, unbuckled his belt, tore off his boots. She got rid of his briefs, stunned by the strong body she'd previously only imagined. "My God." She touched a wound on his abs, suddenly ill when she realized it was from a bullet.

He pushed her back against the pillow, crushing her mouth with his. Emma arched against him, her hands greedily grabbing at him, feeling the strong planes of skin, the cords of muscle. His mouth claimed hers hard, insistent, demanding, and she begged him with her body to give her more.

"Slow," Santana murmured, pulling away. He pushed her hair behind her ears, gazing at her lips, down her neck. "I want this moment to last all night."

He meant it. She saw the hot passion consuming him, felt his need for her. But the moment couldn't last all night, she was too hungry for him. Needed him too much. When he removed her blouse, dropping it to the floor, and snaked his hands around her to unhook her bra, she kissed his shoulder. Found another bullet wound and closed her eyes.

"Santana," she whispered, wanting him inside her now. Needed to feel him, hold him, because this moment had nearly been stolen from them forever.

"I've got you," he said. "Don't worry about anything."

He cupped a breast reverently, shocking her when he tweaked the nipple, bent to suck it into his mouth. She gasped, nearly coming apart from the hot sensations flooding her. Unable to help herself, she reached for him, wrapping her hand around his shaft. He groaned, her nipple still in his mouth, and she felt her body rush with desire only he could sate.

She gasped when he pushed her back against the pillows again, her hand slipping from him. He tore into her breasts with hot kisses, torturing her nipples with expert licks and nibbles that made her cry out. He buried his face against her belly, crushing her to him, his hands tight against her. The groan that ripped from him stole her breath in answer. He slathered her belly with fire, his kisses urgent. He'd come to the top of the lace again, and she arched, unable to help herself, he kissed her through the fabric.

Then shoved the panties away, stripping her bare at last. He kissed her bud, a gentle introduction, then crushed her against his mouth, holding her captive as he tasted her, kissed her. A cry ripped from Emma and his tongue dove inside her, and the climax that hit her felt like it tore her soul apart.

"Santana," she cried out, urging him with her hands.

Gently he placed her against the bed. Finally, she could reach him, and she pulled him toward her.

"Wait," he told her, "I'm going to take care of you."

She realized he was putting on a condom. Her fingers trembling, she tried to help, probably slowing him down instead because he kissed her, pressing her back. His mouth searched hers as if he never wanted to let her go, even as he parted her legs, nestled between them. "You're beautiful," he murmured against her lips, and she cried out when his finger slid inside her, parting her folds. A huge groan escaped him when he encountered her slickness, and Emma arched, begging him silently to come inside her.

At her opening, he stilled, his gaze on hers.

"I want you," she murmured. "I've waited forever for this."

A groan that sounded like a roar ripped from him, and inch by inch, he pushed inside her, claiming her. His fingers danced over her bud, and a wild singing burst inside her as she tried to get closer to the pleasure she felt rising again. Every time her hips convulsed to get more of him, obey the dance of his fingers, he went deeper. A cry gathered at the back of her throat, and he seemed to sense it, because he angled his mouth over hers, kissing her hard. Stealing her breath. Slammed into her over and over, finally letting loose the passion she knew he'd struggled to keep from her. She welcomed it, her hands clutching at his shoulders, begging him not to stop.

The climax broke over her like stars bursting in the skies. "Santana," she cried, wildly tearing at him to bring him closer. His kisses rained against her mouth. She gasped when he clutched her bare bottom in his palms, crushing her, driving himself in deep. With a cry, he collapsed, and she took him in her arms, reveling at the feel of his heartbeat against her.

They lay there boneless, silent. Emma closed her eyes, loving the feel of him in her arms. It had taken years, but she'd finally made love with Santana Dark.

CHAPTER SEVEN

"I've been thinking," Nick said the next day, coming into the barn where Santana was checking over the collection of horses the Dark ranch had amassed over the years. Santana barely glanced at Nick, his mind completely bewitched by the memory of Emma in his arms yesterday. "Your sister doesn't trust me."

That got Santana's attention. He unwillingly met Nick's gaze. "Sierra doesn't trust many people." Santana closed a stall and went to wash his hands in the wide steel double basin sink. "But if I'm being honest, caution's a good thing. You have no reason to trust us, either."

"That's true, except I do."

"A man in your position doesn't get as far as you have by being naïve." Santana toweled off and faced his new boss. "I've no doubt you had us thoroughly checked out. Me, in particular, before you made your offer."

Nick shrugged. "You're right."

"So what's on your mind?"

"Your mother and father adopted all of you because they couldn't have children. According to the paperwork, none of you are related. But Sierra's birth parents are mentioned in the paperwork."

Santana felt strangely like he'd been sucker-punched. "Where did you find that?"

"In the trust information the lawyers had. I've been going over it with them."

He'd never thought about who their biological parents were, hadn't wanted to accept what they'd learned that day in the attorneys' office. Maybe he should have—but they'd all been reeling. Once they knew they no longer had a roof over their head, they'd had to make plans fast.

They'd pushed the heartache away, decided that, blood or no blood, they were a family no one was going to tear apart, and vowed to stay the way they'd always been: close. Tight-knit.

Maybe deep inside they'd known they had to rely on each other. There really had been nowhere else for them to look for emotional security.

"Sierra already thinks I'm some kind of pecuniary weasel. I figure this is your family decision to share or not."

Nick's voice had cracked, like he wasn't comfortable being in the spot he found himself. *Poor bastard.* "Look, for the record, we don't blame you for anything. Dad did what he had to do. He had faults and issues, and a life we never knew about. We're all still processing it. We'll probably be processing it for years. But we don't blame you."

"You may feel that way. Your sister doesn't." Nick sighed.

"Why didn't the lawyers tell her when we were there?"

"Because they just happened to locate a birth certificate

that was hidden inside one of the files. Either someone misfiled it, or it was placed there later. Clerk error. They've worked with your father for years. Papers get lost."

"Why'd they tell you and not Sierra?"

"I asked."

"You asked if any of our birth parents' names were in the files?"

"I wondered how many secrets Sonny had been keeping. And how many my father had been keeping. So I asked, and they checked, and stumbled across a record while the clerk was looking around."

"Why didn't they call Sierra?"

Nick looked tired. Santana felt for him. Their shit wasn't really his problem.

"My guess is they're going to. Or they've tried, and maybe your sister hasn't returned their calls. From the standpoint of the executorship, perhaps they thought it was important to the estate. Hell if I know."

Sierra hadn't said a word to him, but then again, Sierra was notoriously unpredictable about keeping her cell phone on her. She didn't like to carry a purse, just her keys and a Nalgene. Drove him and his brothers nuts.

On the occasion she bothered to find her phone, they got return texts from her, that went, 'k, no, mb for maybe, and ly! for love you(!).

"I'm going to have to think about it." At the moment Sierra was a bit fragile. She was opening a store, which wouldn't be such a crazy idea if she wasn't a twenty-two-year-old who'd never been to college. Sierra had stayed home to take care of the ranch and Sonny, while Santana had ditched as soon as he was out of high school. Almost the day after he'd stolen that kiss from Emma at graduation, he'd found himself on the road, heading to BUD'S.

"Ball's in your court," Nick said, sounding a lot more cheerful now that he'd unloaded the baggage he'd been carrying.

Santana nodded. "Thanks."

"No problem." He looked hopeful. "If you guys have time for dinner tonight, let me know."

He headed out of the barn, whistling, apparently untroubled, now that he'd dumped his startling news on Santana.

Sierra was going to be devastated. Santana didn't know how he was going to tell her.

And he hadn't told Nick the obvious: It was just one more thing Sierra would lay at Nick's door, branding him the most useless wingtip-wearing, striped-suit troublemaker who ever hit Star Canyon.

He left to find the only source of calm he knew, calm he desperately needed right now.

• • •

"Not that I'm trying to make a habit of this," Santana said, "but I figured Joe needed a play date."

They sat on Emma's porch, watching the three dogs run and wrestle in the snow. They'd be wet and muddy, no doubt, but it was worth it to see the three rescues so happy.

"I've got plenty of dog towels just for this kind of occasion," Emma said. "I'm glad you came by."

He hadn't come for a play date, of course. With his

brothers gone, it was just him and Sierra now, and it was lonely at the rental house, which still didn't feel like home.

He tried to tell himself that Joe needed exercise, and it was polite to bring a bottle of wine by and a couple of plates of takeout from Mary's restaurant, considering all that Emma had done for Joe—but that wasn't it, either.

Sitting on this porch with Emma, watching the dogs play, sipping on wine and gazing up at the stars—it felt like a stress-free brain wipe.

No, it wasn't even that.

Something inside him needed to be with her, craved her companionship, wanted to see her smile at him. God, that was the best feeling in the world, when she smiled at him, like he was the only thing that mattered.

He desired Emma, wanted her in the worst way. When they'd made love, he'd been shocked by the depth of his feelings and need for her. But more than that, he just liked being with her.

"Are you still worried about Sierra?" Emma asked.

"I am, and I'm not. She's tough, a survivor. She'll come through it." He pushed away the thought that he hadn't relayed the information from Nick. Part of him had hoped that the attorneys' office would call and tell her, thereby organically relieving him of the problem.

"I guess I meant that she's very focused on her new business."

"Wedding dresses. Impractical, according to Nick, and he's the high roller. I guess he'd know." He sensed Emma was carefully trying to tell him she was worried about Sierra. But he would never accept her taking a job with the fire department.

But wedding dresses—that was an impractical dream destined to fail.

Even Sonny had said his only daughter was spoiled outrageously, and if she hadn't been such a homebody, he thought his daughter would be either a CEO of a large corporation, or riding on the back of a Hell's Angels bike. Coin flip, he'd said, could go either way.

Santana had always detected the note of tender resignation in his father's voice—but Santana himself wasn't equipped to deal with a sister who might be spiraling.

He whistled for Joe, and the Golden retriever ran to him instantly, his tongue heaving. Just seeing that expression brought a smile to Santana's face. "Sierra was right." He patted Joe's head. "This dog is awesome."

Emma smiled, handed him a towel to dry off Joe. She dried Gus and Bean, and all three dogs slurped happily from the water bowl she'd put on the porch. "Come in and we'll eat the food you brought."

He was about to follow her and the dogs into the house when the sound of tires crushing the gravel driveway caught their attention. Sierra's red truck pulled up beside his, and she hopped out. Santana winced at Emma's gasp, but he felt the same.

Sierra's beautiful, waist-length platinum hair was cropped close to her scalp, standing up in a spiky, modern haircut. It wasn't blond anymore, not entirely. Dark streaks of blue mixed in the silvery strands, giving her an entirely modern look.

"Holy shit," he muttered under his breath. "Tell me that's a wig."

"I don't think so," Emma said quickly. "Come on. Act like you love it."

"I don't." He followed Emma as she went to greet Sierra, the pack of dogs bounding along with them. "I don't suppose it would be helpful if I said so."

"I don't think so. Sierra, you're just in time for dinner!"

"Look at my new 'do!" Sierra swiveled her head so they could admire it. "And my new tat!" She pulled up the sleeve of her black top, showing off a long, ornate scroll. Something a warrior might have worn into battle, circa the 1500s. It took up almost the entire inside of her arm.

"Where'd you get the tat?" Santana demanded, pissed and not interested in the design concept. He wanted to know *why*, and what the hell was going on in his sister's head.

"In Lightning Canyon. There's a guy there who everybody was raving about, so I decided to get one!" She looked pleased with herself. "Isn't it beautiful?"

Santana wondered what their father would say if he were alive to see the "new" Sierra. He looked at his sister closely, detecting a shift in her attitude, a new wildness that hadn't been there before. "It's your body," he said gruffly.

"Spoken like a true older brother. Come eat," Emma said, always playing the part of a diplomat, Santana thought.

"I can't. I just came by to show off." Sierra popped her brother on the arm. "How's working for Nick going?"

"It's fine." He was still rattled by the short haircut, tried to tell himself her hair would grow back. She looked like a delighted and mischievous sprite, and he wanted the sister back that he was used to. "We stay out of each other's way."

"I don't know how you stand working for that old donkey. Just being around him gives me ants in my pants!"

She laughed, and gave all the dogs a thorough scratch around their ears before getting in her truck. "I'm going to look at a space in town to put my store. I'll pick up some doughnuts for breakfast!"

She waved and drove off, still grinning. Santana turned to Emma. "Did we discuss whether I was still worried about my crazy little sister?"

Emma laughed. "Come on. Hot food and maybe a toddy will make you feel better."

"It won't," he grumbled, willingly following. The dogs led the way, churning snow and keeping an eye out for things to chase in the snow. "She looks like a boy that painted his hair."

"She looked darling."

They dried the dogs off again and went inside the house. "I sense you're saying that to help me get over the shock."

She poured them both another glass of wine and pulled the food out from the oven where she'd kept it warming. "Sierra's just expressing herself."

He sank onto a seat at the island, watching Emma. The dogs had settled themselves onto their dog beds, worn out from playing. Princess the cat eyed him from the top of a bookcase. The gray lovebirds slept perched together. This place should be a hotbed of disorganization, a zoo, but it was calm and comforting. Like Emma.

Santana felt worn out from trying to digest his sister's appearance. "Dad loved Sierra's hair."

"Change is good. It's okay, Santana." She smiled at him, put a plate in front of him that he had no desire to touch. "Obviously she needed to do that."

"I guess." He drummed his fingers on the granite island

top. "She's so beautiful. Why is she making herself ugly on purpose?"

"Santana." Emma giggled, shaking her head at him. "She's twenty-two and full of spirit. She's expressing herself. Why is short hair ugly on her and not on you?"

He stared at her. "I'm a guy?"

"Oh, and men like long hair, therefore, Sierra must conform to that beauty ideal?" She sat beside him. "Your sister is adorable. Don't worry, someday her prince will find her, and he will love her for the beautiful girl she is, inside and out."

"I like your hair just the way it is," he said gruffly, eying the red top-knot of hair curling out of the ponytail holder. He loved Emma's hair, loved the springy, bounciness of it. It was sexy as hell. What if Sierra sparked a revolution in Star Canyon of boyish hair styles, and Emma followed suit? "You won't do that, will you?"

She looked at him. "Would it matter?"

Maybe he should be making changes, be a little more Sierra and a lot less Santana, looking for a past that wasn't coming back. What the hell was wrong with him? "I'd still be here as often as you'd let me be."

She smiled at him, and he perked up. It was like the sun breaking through clouds when she smiled at him, like he was the only man on the planet.

Suddenly, he knew he had to wake up to that smile every day for the rest of his life.

"I'm not cutting my hair, or getting a tattoo. Though I respect Sierra and support her for following her inner guide."

"I don't care," he said, "be bald, be beautiful. Whatever you want. Just kiss me, Emma Glass."

Emma slid off the stool and into Santana's arms without hesitation. "I thought you'd never ask."

He sought her mouth hungrily, was surprised when she met him kiss for kiss. Her arms slipped around his neck, pulling him close, drawing him in—and suddenly, Santana realized that this kiss was different.

It was urgent, no holds barred.

Holy shit, she was trying to tell him she wanted him to make love to her. At least that's what he thought she was trying to tell him, but a man never knew—

"I can feel you over-thinking again."

"I am." He groaned as she pressed closer. All he wanted to do was grab her up and take her. He was harder than he'd ever been, aching to possess her.

She slid a hand up his chest. "Make love to me, Santana."

He heard wind rushing past him. "Are you sure?"

She looked up at him, raised a brow. "Are you afraid this is becoming a thing? That all the rumors in Star Canyon won't be rumors anymore?"

He didn't—couldn't—think about anything but her. He stripped off her top even as she was working on his, her fingers furiously undoing buttons as they kissed. God, he could kiss her all night—but then her fingers slid down his back and reached for his zipper, and he thought *God, I could do this all night, too.*

The bra went somewhere and all he could do was stare. "You're beautiful," he said reverently, but she didn't allow him any time to process how beautiful she was because her hands were in his briefs, and he was harder than he'd ever been in his life. "Bed? Table? Chair?" he gasped out.

"Bed so we don't scandalize the pets," she said, and he

knew she was teasing him, but he didn't care. He swept her into his arms, striding down the hall with her, as she giggled against his chest.

He bounced onto the bed with her, and Emma squealed, laughing. She tugged off his jeans, made short work of his briefs, and then there was nothing between them but the tiniest piece of pink string he'd ever seen. "I'm going to have a coronary right here."

"Santana—"

"No, no. No over-thinking. Hang on, gorgeous, just give me one second to process this much beauty."

She lay back against the pillows, the slight chill in the room puckering her nipples and goose-pimpling her skin. Her body was one smooth ribbon of feminine beauty, accented by the pink excuse for a panty.

Then her hand closed around his erection, and Santana nearly blacked out from the sudden heat swamping him. He took her hands in his, placing her arms above her head so she couldn't torture him. He claimed her mouth, loving hearing her gasp underneath him. Kissed her long and thoroughly until she writhed beneath him.

But the breasts, ah, he had to taste them. He kissed her there, taking the nipple of each round globe into his mouth, teasing it with his tongue.

"Santana," she murmured, and he released her hands so he could tease her nipples as he kissed down her belly. Her stomach was so flat and smooth, the skin so soft.

The thong provided no resistance at all, and he teased her, tasting her, groaning when she cried out his name again. To his surprise, she climaxed quickly—too quickly.

"Santana!" She pulled at his hair, his shoulders, anything

to get him closer to her, inside her. But it wasn't enough. He wanted more.

"Shhh, baby girl," he told her, taking her in his arms. "Let me please you."

He kissed her, stroking between her legs with his fingers, teasing her clit, her wetness driving him mad. It was all he could do to hold himself back from getting inside her. He teased her nipples, circled her bud as he felt her body tightening against his—and when she begged him to make her come, he slipped inside her, bringing a cry of pleasure from her that could have been heard in the next county and nearly making him explode right then.

He made a superhuman effort, squeezing his eyes shut, wanting it to last forever. Draw out her pleasure.

"Oh, God, Santana," she whispered against his mouth, riding against him hard. She was tight, so tight, so ready for him. Her body was made for his. And the fact that she wanted him so urgently was blinding hot, robbing him of speech and anything but the need to keep plunging inside her. Her hands pulled at him, pressing him closer to her—but when she wrapped her legs around his waist, dragging him deep inside her and imprisoning him in the softness of her body, Santana broke with a cry, coming hard, his heart pounding so hard it felt like it might rip right out of him.

He collapsed, and she held him, and just for a moment, Santana felt lost. His heart was still racing, but Emma's arms were around him, centering him.

He didn't know what to say. Jesus, what did a guy say after a mind-bending experience like that? *Thank you? I think I just saw the thrones of Heaven? Give me twenty minutes and let me do it again, I swear I can do better than two orgasms for my lady?*

"Are you all right?" Emma asked, and he smiled when she giggled.

"I'm fine. But I think the dogs are worried."

The sound of snuffling noses under the door crack made both of them laugh. "They think I'm hurting you."

"They think something," Emma said, rising to kiss him, "but you definitely didn't hurt me."

"Good," he said gruffly. He wasn't sure exactly what had just happened—or how it had happened.

She'd asked him to make love to her. Just like the last time, which he'd feared might never happen again. He'd had a miracle visited on him, after all these years.

"Emma, marry me," he said, shocking himself.

She tossed a pillow at him. "Let's go walk the dogs. Then I need to go to bed." Her tone was uncomfortable, suddenly awkward.

He wanted to say *let's skip the walk and stay in bed*, but selfish bastards never won fair ladies, so he pulled on his jeans. "I'll walk them. And then I'll let you get some sleep."

"I had surgeries today, and one farm emergency in the morning, so I guess I'm a little tired." He handed her the bra that had somehow gotten caught in his jeans. She handed him his briefs which had landed on the bedside table. "Santana, I know what this is. Don't worry. No proposal is necessary. That's not what I'm looking for."

He pulled on his jeans. "Okay." What was she looking for? "What was it?"

"This?" She smiled. "It was wonderful."

Was she telling him not to over-think this, either? How could he not? "Maybe I want to over-think it."

Snouts nosed at the crack of the door and the hardwood

floor. Emma shrugged into her bra, and he watched, fascinated. "You have beautiful breasts. Did I tell you that? Because the whole time I was making love to you, I thought I was telling you how beautiful you are. Every curve of you, every inch of you, is so beautiful that I swear it nearly stopped my heart."

She stopped dressing, looked at him. "Thank you."

He wanted her again, already. The snouts weren't to be denied, though—and he felt hesitation from Emma. Maybe even some distance.

He wanted to break through that resistance, that wall she'd constructed, with all his might. But he didn't know why it was suddenly there.

What if this was it? What if she never let him make love to her again? What if he never got inside that soft, welcoming body, heard her cry his name over and over?

Oh, holy, *holy* shit. It was because he'd blurted out that proposal. He'd scared her. He hadn't been able to help it. His mouth had only said what his subconscious was thinking. Once you'd seen the promised land, it wasn't like you'd keep looking for a better promised land.

"I'll walk the dogs," he said, opening the door, and the two shepherd puppies and Joe raced in, swirling tails and anxious faces looking for Emma. She patted them, and they engulfed her, delighted now that they had her full attention.

And damn their furry hides, he knew exactly how they felt.

CHAPTER EIGHT

"It was dumb," Nick said, "I know it was dumb. But when I found your sister hauling stuff out of the storage barn at night, piece by piece, and putting it in her truck to haul away, I had to do something. I know the trust said that everything except strictly personal items like clothes were to be left as part of the ranch estate." He sighed deeply. "Look, she thought she was stealing from me, and the stuff obviously meant a hell of a lot to her, so I told her to take it. She's a pack rat, I guess." He shrugged. "What was I supposed to do with it, anyway? And then, I thought about it, and I wanted to help her. Somehow. So I offered to finance her business."

Santana told himself to listen and not throw a punch. He sat on a hay bale and waited for more of the story.

"Okay, I'm not saying loaning your sister money—"

"She calls it a bet."

Nick looked embarrassed. "Maybe it is a bet. The terms are technical and not necessarily legal."

"Did you sign papers? If you signed paperwork, it's

legal, and my sister is tied to losing money to you." There was a great chance he wasn't going to be able to work for Nick without doing the man bodily harm. "Who the hell gets involved in a venture with a twenty-two-year-old girl who has no college degree and little life experience outside of this town? My sister isn't a world traveler like you, Nick. She's not a heavy hitter in the world of finance." The whole thing felt so slimy. "And now I know that you're cast from the same mold as your old man."

Nick sat on a bale across from him. "Santana, your sister isn't the little girl you think she is."

"Watch it, or your tongue will find itself out of your mouth."

Nick scowled. "Would you quit giving me shit? For your information, while I may not be a Navy SEAL, I'm pretty confident I can take you."

Santana was so surprised he laughed out loud. He shook his head at his wiry, suit-wearing cousin. Nick had been on his way out to catch a flight——private jet, of course—when Santana had waylaid him, determined to beat his hide blue for taking advantage of Sierra. "I don't think so. You could try, but it wouldn't end well."

Nick shook his head. "I don't want to fight with you. Look, drive me to the airport. I'll explain it to you."

"You're the boss-man." He meant to sound dismissive, but Nick's attention was on his cell phone.

"Thanks. If you drive, I can get some of these calls out of the way."

"I'm not a flunky. I'm not a driver, either, or a taxi service. I'm a hand."

"I know, sorry. Anyway, you want to hear about your

sister and her escapades, give me a ride. Otherwise, this chapter will have to wait until next week."

"Would your highness like me to pack a cooler of water bottles and your favorite adult beverage?"

"Thanks." Nick had already turned toward the Range Rover. Santana told himself that his cousin wasn't a man on whom sarcasm worked well, and grabbed a couple of water bottles out of the barn fridge. Nick tossed him the keys. "Where is Sierra, anyway?"

"At home with Joe. I think they're looking through some wedding books, last I checked." Disgruntled, Santana got into the driver's seat. "I'm not wearing a cap, I'm not carrying your luggage, and I'm not doing anything except driving you to the airport."

Nick glanced up, strapping himself into the seat belt as he looked at Santana. "A driver's uniform would look good on you. I always think it's good to play the part, don't you?"

Santana was about to bean him, until he saw Nick's eyes twinkling. "You're a laugh a minute. Where to?"

"DFW. I'm heading out to London for a couple of days."

That would give him a nice distance to pick apart the lies Nick was probably about to tell as a cover story. He drove through the center of Star Canyon, astounded when he saw Sierra and Emma dragging a mannequin from a truck bed. The girls hoisted it up, carrying it down the street toward Sierra's shop like it was some kind of trophy. "Just a second."

"No problem." Nick eyed the women. "Glad to see Sierra is taking this bet seriously."

"You shut up until I get all the information out of you I want. I'm not happy with you at all." Mannequins weren't cheap, and Sierra was pouring money into a losing venture.

He pulled in front of the store and got out. "What are you doing?"

"Carrying our sacrifice to the moon goddess. What does it look like?" Sierra demanded.

"Let me." He took the mannequin from them, holding it in one arm. "Open the door."

"What are you doing with *him*?" Sierra asked.

"What are you doing with *her*?" Santana asked Emma. "Why aren't you at the clinic?"

"It's my lunch break."

"My sister is getting you involved in a questionable scheme."

"I don't do questionable schemes," Nick said, coming inside the empty shop. "Why is it questionable? Isn't Sierra reliable?"

"Does she look reliable?" He pointed to the eyebrow ring, the tat, and the wild hair.

Sierra smacked his finger away. "Quit being a douche! You've had a serious crimp in your brain for days, Santana."

He looked at Emma, who shrugged, her smile sympathetic. She thought he had a crimp, too—and he did, all thanks to her. It was like she was sucking everything out of his brain that was cold hearted and mechanical, and he missed the old Santana. The old Santana had lived on instinct and razor-sharp focus. The old Santana would never have blurted out a proposal. Why had he messed up what had been turning into the only beautiful thing currently in his life?

"I thought you were going to kick Nick's ass," Emma said. "That's what you said yesterday when you left the table."

Nick looked interested in this. "I told him I could take him. He decided to be a lover and not a fighter."

They all laughed at the disgust written on Santana's face. "I reserve the right to harm you after I hear your story."

Sierra ushered both men to the door. "You're bothering me and Emma. I only have her during her lunch hour. So you boys are going to have to go play forts and battle stations elsewhere."

"Come with us," Nick said.

Sierra stopped. "Why?"

"To protect me from your brother?"

Sierra wouldn't fall for that line, would she? Santana watched this exchange with interest, fraternal protection rising inside him.

"You're a land shark. You don't need protection." Sierra grabbed her coat. "But I'll go. You probably shouldn't be alone together. No telling what romance might spring up."

"Join us," Santana said to Emma. "I need protection from my boss and my sister."

"Yeah, come along," Nick said. "I'll spring for lunch somewhere."

"I thought we were going to be late to the airport. You have a flight to catch to London," Santana said.

"I do, but my pilot just moved the flight plan back. So I have about forty-five minutes to kill."

"I probably could," Emma said. "I don't have any more appointments this afternoon."

Sierra clapped her hands. "There's a place in Lightning Canyon that's having an estate sale, and I heard—from Mary, who is quite reliable—that there's a vintage wedding dress there that would be perfect for my collection! Let's stop in and look at it. It'll be an adventure!"

Santana looked at Nick. "It's your popsicle stand she's running."

"We'll stop," Nick said after a moment. "It can't take more than a minute to see an old dress."

"Old dress? You mean vintage. There's a difference." Sierra locked up the shop and elbowed Nick as they walked toward his car. "Semantics are important, right? Otherwise you'd be a salesman instead of a businessman. Or as Santana calls you, our land shark relation."

Santana glanced at Emma, who looked away, clearly awkward around him.

He'd really spooked her.

Hell, I really spooked myself.

• • •

"How did Mary hear about this estate sale?" Emma asked, staring up at the rundown Victorian. It had turned grey with age, its once-white porch and gingerbread trim now cast with a dirty somberness. The windows were bright and clean, though, and the magnolia trees out front looked healthy, despite the chilly winter day. People milled in and out of the old grand lady, carrying their spoils from the estate. There'd been a mile of cars parked down the narrow, dirt-packed road. Emma was amazed that so many people would have known about this house and its contents. There wasn't another house around for what seemed like miles, its position in the countryside remote though accessible.

"A cousin of hers owned the place, one Melly Shelby.

Mary said Melly took care of everyone around here during the Depression, and if it hadn't been for her, folks in this area might not have eaten." Sierra looked thrilled to be making the detour, the men less so. Nick seemed amused, but he always wore a slightly-amused expression. It was a shame he'd come into the family on such devastating terms, Emma thought. Santana's face was wreathed in a scowl, glowering at his sister for dragging them out here on a fool's errand, and at Nick, for being, well, the instrument of their downfall, probably. Or maybe Santana scowled at Nick because they were total opposites in personality.

"Come on," she whispered to Santana, "it will only take five minutes."

"This whole wedding thing is insanity. Sierra needs to go to work at Mary's restaurant. Someplace where she can draw a consistent wage."

"Let's go see what your sister has found," Emma said, trying to get his mind off Sierra's madcap lifestyle.

"Why we want a wedding dress that's no doubt fifty years old, judging by the look of this place," Santana said, "is a mystery to me. Don't those things turn yellow after a few years? It'll look like a yellowed mummy wrapping."

"Is he always Mr. Positive?" Nick asked Sierra.

"He's not into wedding stuff. Marriage in general is for foolish men who stupidly exchange their freedom for the chains of fidelity and matrimony," Sierra said, studying a photo on a wall.

Emma's gaze met Santana's, her eyes wide at Sierra's words. The proposal he'd uttered created distance she wanted to close but couldn't. He hadn't meant to propose— or if he had, their marriage would be an impulse that wouldn't stand the test of time. Yet she'd been unable to stop thinking about it, certain he wasn't in love with her, wishing that he was somehow. "Hey, Emma, I think this is a photo of Mary when she was young, and probably Melly Shelby. That's definitely Mary. I'd know that brave smile anywhere," Sierra said.

"I've never known much about Mary." Emma looked close, glad for a chance to escape the intensity of Santana's gaze. "I mean, we've known her all our lives, but she's just always been the owner of the Midnight Bar and Grill."

"The lady who sits in the third pew in church, and looks at you askance if you take her seat," Sierra said.

"Mary makes the best chicken fried chicken around," Santana said. "You two are focusing on the wrong things." He leaned close to look, and Emma could smell his skin and something woodsy.

"We need to move along," Nick said, "if I'm springing for your lunch, kids."

"And we brought you along just for that reason," Sierra said brightly. "Look!" Sierra stopped, completely transfixed. "There it is!"

At the end of the hallway, the gown rested on an old fashioned dressmaker's bust, and Emma could tell at once the dress was in pristine condition. It had obviously looked been stored away carefully and lovingly, waiting for its magical day to arrive.

"It's beautiful," Sierra said reverently.

Emma had to agree. "The lace on the cap sleeves is stunning. I think it's hand-made."

The gown had a simple Victorian bodice that tied at the rib cage, a high waistline that would give the wearer a turn-of-the-century look. The entire dress was made of lace, which had been worked into flowers.

A curator came over when she noticed their interest. "This is Miss Melly Shelby's wedding dress," she said. "Of course she never married, so this lovely gown has never been worn."

"Never?" Emma asked, suddenly feeling sorry for lonely Miss Shelby.

"No. She made this, working the lace herself." The curator reminisced. "Of course, when we were in school, Melly Shelby was voted Most Popular, Most Beautiful, and Most Likely to Succeed. She definitely succeeded in her life. She just never found the man of her dreams. Excuse me."

The curator floated off to help some other customers.

"Just like Mary," Emma said. "Mary will probably never marry either."

"Ew, I get chills thinking about poor Miss Shelby making her dream dress, and then never getting to wear it. Look, I've got goose pimples."

"That's because it's twenty degrees in this rickety joint," Santana said. "Let's get out of here."

Nick chuckled. "I'm warm as toast."

The ladies glared at Santana.

"Oh, all right," he said, relenting. "Shall we have tea here?"

"No." Sierra waved the curator back over. "We'll take it. This gentleman right here," she said, indicating Nick, "will pay for it."

Emma watched as Nick pulled out his wallet. Her gaze bounced to Santana, surprised that Nick did exactly what Sierra said.

"Let's go outside," Santana told her. "I promise it's warmer out there."

She followed him out of the house. "Was that weird? Or was it my imagination?"

"Of course it's weird. Sierra's training Nick. So far, I'd say she has him wrapped around her finger." Santana sat on the porch and leaned back on his elbows, untroubled by his sister's methods.

The cold from the porch seeped through Emma's jeans to her fanny. "I don't know what to think about Sierra's dress shop."

"It doesn't matter what anyone thinks. It's happening." He leaned back. "It's on Nick, the way I figure it. Whatever their bet is, I hope he knows what he's up against."

Sierra bounded out onto the porch, Nick following behind her, holding the long dress in a plastic bag. "All done!"

"This was quite the adventure. So much history in this little town," Nick said.

Santana got up. "Here's the thing, Nick. Buying my sister rags and hiring me, financing my sister's pipe dream—we don't need any of this. We're not a charity case. You're not responsible for us, and frankly, we don't need another family member. Especially one who owns everything we had."

"Santana!" Surprised, Emma grabbed his arm. "Come on. Let's get Nick to the airport."

The two men glared at each other for a moment. Santana hadn't moved, though she tried to guide him away from Nick. What if they came to blows? That wasn't going to help the situation.

Then again, what difference did it make? She was the only true outsider here. Releasing Santana, she stalked off the porch. "If you two want to fight, have at it. I'm getting in the car. It's too cold to stand around and listen to stubborn men squabble."

Santana was right: Sierra's dream was a bit outlandish, but that wasn't her problem. Nick was trying to buy his way into the Dark family, but that too didn't concern her. And Santana was just being…well, he was being an annoying hardheaded male. Unfortunately, the only time he was sweet was in bed.

That wasn't going to be enough.

CHAPTER NINE

They were walking to the Range Rover when Nick got a call on his cell phone. The three of them waited for him to finish his call, Santana wondering what he was doing here playing gofer to a man who had just bankrolled Sierra's shop.

"My flight is canceled," Nick said, rejoining them. "A snowstorm came in unexpectedly." He glanced up at the sky, searching the overcast whiteness. "Do we get much snow in Star Canyon?"

"We?" Santana sighed. The man was part of Star Canyon, whether he liked it or not. Nick seemed nothing if not determined. "No more than six inches, most likely. But it's a good time to head back if you're not going to the airport. Am I driving?"

"Sure," Nick said. "I can work if you drive."

"Has someone ferried you all your life? Driven you here, flown you there?" Santana asked, more curious than annoyed.

"I never really thought about it." Nick shrugged.

"While you two butt antlers to see who's the strongest, can we get in? It's cold," Sierra said.

"If I'm driving, Emma's sitting up front with me. She's the only person among us who doesn't annoy the crap out of me."

"Fair enough." Nick opened the back door. Sierra got into the car carefully with her purchase. She spread it over her knees. "Never mind him, Emma. Just ignore the driver if he gets too ornery." She glared at Nick. "Just because we're stuck together for a couple of hours back here doesn't mean we're friends."

"Of course not," Nick said, amused. "Business partners, only."

"That's right."

Emma got in next to him, and Santana felt himself relax slightly. "Hungry?"

"Starving."

"How do you feel about grabbing a bite?" Santana asked in the general direction of the backseat.

"I'm hungry," Nick said.

"I don't care," Sierra said. "I can go days without food. But if you folks want to stop somewhere, the curator suggested Miss Sugar's Tea room. She apparently also operates a popular B&B."

"That's not food," Santana said. "Cookies and tea aren't going to cut it."

"You don't always need a steak," Sierra said. "For your information, Mr. Narrowminded, Miss Sugar apparently serves a wicked BLT."

"What is it with all the spinsters in this town?" Santana

asked. "Will we have to listen to the sad tales of the never-married over our BLTs?"

"He's a spoilsport, Emma," Sierra said. "Jeez, Santana, what a crab you are sometimes."

Santana liked the sound of Emma's laughter at Sierra's comment, even if it was at his expense. "You're okay with the tea room?" Santana asked her.

"Sure. I'll eat anything."

He thought she was always much more easygoing than he was. Santana told himself it was watching Nick buy the wedding gown for Sierra that had him in a twist, but more likely, it was Emma. He wanted to be alone with her, kiss her, hold her.

"Miss Sugar's it is," he said, and drove into town while Emma looked the directions up on her phone.

"Apparently, Miss Sugar is the local authority on ghosts," Sierra said, thrilled to be supping with the supernatural. "She has so many tales of transformative incidents she's been asked to write a book on the subject!"

"Ridiculous," Nick said, and Santana thought that was the first time he'd agreed with him on any topic.

"What do you think, Emma?" Santana asked.

"I don't think it's ridiculous," Emma said. "I never doubt the spirits."

"You're too levelheaded to believe in ghosts," he said.

"You're too thick-headed not to," Sierra said. "We've had this discussion a time or two over the years. My brother isn't a believer. Nor am I, for that matter."

"We have to believe," Emma said. "Otherwise, if we have no connection to the supernatural, we're not allowing for miracles in our lives."

Santana thought he'd experienced a few miracles, the most recent being making love to her. That was a miracle he hoped happened again, and soon. He would willingly shop for gowns, and eat spinster-made BLTs, if it meant he could lose himself in her sweet welcoming body. Had he prayed for heavenly assistance when he was in war zones overseas? Yeah. A fucking lot. And their father had been religious as hell. What was there to believe in now? "I don't know," he said instead.

"This is fascinating," Nick said. "I was at a party once where there was a fortune teller as the evening's entertainment. Everyone seemed quite taken with her."

"And taken by her. I'm sure she emptied plenty of purses while she was there," Santana said.

"You say purses like it was a female event. But the men listened, too. Skeptically, at first," Nick continued. "In my case, she told me that my ambition would one day bring me down."

Emma turned to look at him. "Bad party tricks, obviously? You don't seem like such an ambitious man to me."

"I don't know," Nick said softly. "Her words made me cautious. Ever since that night, I've felt this strange sensation that any minute I might walk into more than I can handle."

"What a load," Santana said. "If you let nonsense like that into your head, I doubt very seriously your ability to keep a working ranch together."

"That's what I have you for," Nick said.

He felt Emma's gaze on him. "He's right. You need him, and he needs you," she said.

There was an instant recoil in Santana's gut, even as he realized the truth of Emma's words.

"We don't *need* anybody," Sierra said. "We could live in a cave and be perfectly happy."

"You could," Emma said quietly, "but you're not. Nick is financing your business. And you're helping him hold on to the land he has zero idea about working. As far as business matchups go, you both need each other."

Sierra sighed gustily. "It doesn't mean we have to sit around thinking self-defeating ideas like we need each other. Jeez. What ever happened to the pioneer spirit of raising yourself up? Relying on yourself?"

"I don't care about independence," Nick said, stunning Santana. "I'm happy to be with family."

"We're not your family," Sierra said. "You've adopted us, but that's as far as the ties go."

"Your fathers were brothers," Emma said. "Even if there's no blood tie, you're in this together for the time being."

"Ah, nuts." Sierra poked Santana in the shoulder. "If you marry her, one half of your marriage will be rational and steeped in common sense. Here's a hint: it won't be your side."

"No one's getting married," Emma said, before Santana could reply. What shocked him was that he hadn't been about to make the response Emma had, which should have been his, as the typical male response. Don't tie me down—right?

No, the words on his lips had been *No, her side has all the brains and the beauty.*

What the hell was his problem?

"Anyway," Sierra said, "you're all way too serious. There's no such thing as magic, or supernatural elements. It's all talk.

It starts when you're a kid, because your parents want you to believe in stuff to make you behave." She grinned. "I'm not even sure I believe in God," Sierra continued. "Definitely I don't believe in angels, saints, ghosts, spirits. I just don't."

"And yet you're opening a store you've named the Magic Wedding Dress?" Nick asked. "I saw the sign in the back of the storeroom. And the business cards."

"I didn't say I didn't believe in great sales technique," Sierra said. "That old woman gave me a great idea. I'm running with it. I'm going to put that antique dress in the front window and never sell it. It's my good luck charm. Melly Shelby may never have married, but her beautiful dress will bring me lots of ladies who will want a gown as amazing as hers."

"I think her dress meant something to her," Santana said. "She didn't make it to be a good luck charm."

"And I think you have a soft heart, especially when it concerns elderly folk with a hard luck story, and little children who need role models," Sierra told him.

"Sierra!" Astonished by the cold note in Sierra's voice, Emma turned to look at her best friend. "What has gotten into you?"

"I don't know," Sierra said glumly. "I don't feel very well."

"What's wrong?" Nick asked, concerned.

"We'll get you some lunch," Santana pulled in to Miss Sugar's. "That'll probably help. We'll have to hurry, though. I don't want to get caught on the road if the snow starts."

He studied Sierra as she got out of the truck. She was pale, but that wasn't what caught his attention. It was how carefully Nick hung the wedding dress from a hook in the back, laying it over the seat, then hurrying around to put a hand under Sierra's elbow. Santana thought his sister would probably give Nick a swift kick to the ankle, but she didn't.

In fact, his starchy sister sort of melted against Nick for support.

"Let's get you out of the cold," he told her, taking his sister from Nick and guiding her inside the cheery tearoom.

Sierra was hot, very hot. Santana touched his sister's forehead as a tall woman—maybe Miss Sugar?—yelled at them from the direction of what he supposed was the kitchen to take any seat they wanted, and she'd be with them in a moment. "Sit down, Sierra." He guided her into a funky star-shaped chair at the nearest table. "When did you start running a fever?"

"I'm not," Sierra said. "At least, I wasn't."

"You are now." He felt her head again. "Let's get you out of your jacket."

He helped Sierra shrug out of her big parka. Nick took a seat, his face helpless and worried.

"Let me see." Emma knelt down next to him, staring up at Sierra. She touched her friend's forehead. "Sierra, you were fine at the estate sale."

"I know." Sierra took a deep breath. "I just feel so strange all of a sudden."

"Maybe we should drive on back," Nick said.

"Let's get her some water at least," Emma suggested.

The large woman who'd bellowed at them cheerily came over, her face wreathed with delight to have customers. They were the only ones in the place, and Santana wondered about the veracity of Miss Sugar's being the most popular café in town. "Hello, folks. Sorry about the wait. I was putting the last bit of frosting on a cake that had just cooled. Strawberry cake with cream cheese frosting, in case you're wondering. And I made a blackberry pie." She looked down at Sierra's flushed face. Santana thought the woman was maybe too thin to eat much of her own baking. She had white hair she'd twisted in a long braid that hung over her shoulder and snaked down to her rib cage. Her white apron was clean, and lettered with blue letters that matched the tearoom décor: *Miss Sugar*.

"Miss Sugar," Santana said, "could we have some water?"

"With some lemon," Sierra said. "I'm craving a lemon."

"You sick, honey?" Miss Sugar asked.

"I wasn't ten minutes ago," Sierra said faintly.

"I'll get that water." Miss Sugar beetled off quickly.

Sierra's hands were shaking. Santana took one in his, stunned that it was ice-cold. "Sierra, you're really ill."

"Did you eat something while we were at the estate sale? I saw some plates of cookies sitting out," Emma asked.

"I didn't."

"Are you hurting anywhere?" Emma said, and Santana was glad for her levelheaded approach. He was far too worried about his little sister to be any good with this. But he couldn't remember Sierra ever being sick—and it troubled him. She'd had the odd cold over the years, and once they'd all gotten the chickenpox together, creating quite a bit of mayhem in the house for their mom because they'd been fairly demanding patients.

But not Sierra. She'd laid quietly in the room with her brothers, where they'd set up camp in the den so Mom could oversee them all at once. Sierra alone had kept a cheerful countenance, when she wasn't asleep.

She'd gotten well first, too.

"I'm not in any pain. Not even a headache," Sierra said. "I'm never sick. But I don't feel good at all."

"Okay. Let's get some water in her, maybe a to-go cup, too, and try to outrun the storm," Nick suggested. "She'd feel better in her own bed."

"I want a slice of that pie," Sierra said. "And I want to hear at least one of Miss Sugar's ghost stories."

"You don't even believe in ghosts," Nick said. "Why would you care to hang around to listen to baloney?"

"I don't know," Sierra said weakly. "Is anybody else hearing chimes?"

Santana pressed his sister back in the chair and stood as Miss Sugar came back to the table with her tray, rapidly putting four waters, a bowl of sliced lemons, and a platter of tiny wafer cookies on the table.

"Thank you," Sierra said, her voice dull. "Can I have a slice of that pie and a cup of hot tea?"

"Sierra," Santana cautioned, and Nick added, "In to-go containers, if possible."

Miss Sugar touched Sierra's forehead. "My, you're burning up, young lady."

"I feel like crap," Sierra said.

"Did this just come on?" Miss Sugar asked.

"Yes." Sierra sipped her water after Nick squeezed a generous lemon slice in it.

"I wonder if you'd be interested in trying a cure," Miss Sugar said.

"A cure?" Santana asked, raising a brow.

"A remedy, to be more precise."

"Sure," Sierra said.

"What kind of remedy?" Emma asked quickly.

"A natural remedy, don't worry." Miss Sugar went off, and Santana glanced at Emma.

"It can't hurt, I suppose," Emma said.

"Whatever it takes to hear her ghost story," Sierra said.

"Since when are you so interested in local legends?" Santana asked.

"I don't know." Sierra took a lemon slice and ate it, rind and all. She took another lemon slice and downed that as well.

"Sierra," Santana said, "since when do you gobble lemons?"

"I'm craving citrus. I can't explain it."

Miss Sugar returned, setting down a piece of pie for Sierra and the hot tea. She also gave her a water bottle. "Drink that first. Divide the bottle in four parts, and drink a fourth every fifteen minutes."

"That pie is beautiful," Sierra said. "I feel better already."

Miss Sugar smiled. "You'll feel fine soon. What can I get the rest of you folks?"

"I'll have a BLT," Emma said. "I hear yours are delicious."

"Good." She looked at Santana. "And you, sir?"

"Shouldn't we be hitting the road?" Santana asked, glancing at Nick.

"Maybe if Sierra gets some food in her, she'll feel better," Nick said. "We can take thirty minutes to eat and get out before the snow starts falling." He also ordered a BLT, and Santana sighed. Sierra was drinking her water, just as prescribed, and ogling her pie, so he also ordered one of the infamous BLTs. Although how amazing could a BLT be? Bacon, lettuce, tomato, big deal.

"Me, too, please," Sierra said, and Miss Sugar went off, delighted to have four orders for her much-lauded BLTs.

Sierra dumped a ton of sugar in her hot tea, squeezed a large slice of lemon in it, devoured the slice when she'd squeezed all the juice from it, and forked a piece of the pie. "I'm sorry, folks. I hate to eat in front of you, but I'm trying this. It's calling my name."

"I'm glad to see you have an appetite." Emma took a wafer from the cookie tray. "We can probably rule out appendicitis."

"Maybe it was something in that house." Nick drank his water.

"This is so good it's sinful." Sierra sighed happily. "I'm taking home a whole pie if she's got one!"

Miss Sugar returned with their BLTs, setting a plate down in front of each of them. Santana had never seen such huge sandwiches. Each BLT was a masterpiece in its own right, towering with bacon and tomato layers, generous cups of mayo on the side. The bread was a crustless, soft egg-style, looking cut from a fresh loaf.

"You're sure you want to eat more, Sierra?" Emma asked, watching Sierra tear into the BLT with gusto.

"I'm feeling better," Sierra said. She picked up the bottle of water with the so-called "remedy" in it. "This stuff must be working."

"Clearly a placebo effect," Santana muttered.

"Whatever. It's working," Sierra said cheerfully. "And this BLT lives up to its reputation!"

Emma smiled at Santana. It was a look meant to calm him, reassure him that his little sister would be fine.

She would be. He knew that. They all would be.

"Snow's starting to fall," Miss Sugar said, happily reappearing at their table. "How's the food, folks?"

"Delightful," Nick said. "You might bring me the bill. We need to hit the road."

"You won't be going anywhere today," Miss Sugar said, her face suddenly woeful.

"Oh?" Nick raised an imperious brow, his voice suddenly quite cold. The change in Friendly Nick to what was probably Boardroom Nick even startled Sierra, who glanced at him, her eyes huge.

"No, I'm afraid not." Miss Sugar couldn't have been more sympathetic. "Not if that's your black car outside."

Of course it was Nick's black car. They'd been the only people to park in the six spaces in front of Miss Sugar's tearoom.

"Is there a problem?" Nick demanded, his tone icy.

"Looks like a tire thief came by," Miss Sugar said, maybe not quite as sympathetic as she should be, Santana thought. "We've had a gang working our small town. They come by with a truck to toss the tires into and make short work of it. Can have your tires off in less than twelve seconds, just like at NASCAR."

Nick got up, his body stiff, visibly annoyed. Santana stared at him, surprised by the change in the affable Nick. They walked with him to the window to see the damage. Nick let out a word Santana had never heard him use before as he saw his car sitting on cinder blocks, the wheels and tires vanished.

"Why haven't you called the sheriff?" Nick demanded.

"I did," Miss Sugar said, offended. "Of course I did immediately, before I even knew if that was your car! We try to stay one step ahead of that gang!"

"Well, you're not staying one step ahead," Nick said

curtly. "I'm sure you have someone in town who conveniently tends to this type of occurrence?"

"I beg your pardon," Miss Sugar said. "If you are suggesting, sir, that we thieve tires in this town to make a bit of cash from unsuspecting travelers, I assure you that's the last thing anyone would want here. We want our visitors to return. Any good business person knows that. And for your information, since the theft occurred on my property, lunch is on me."

She sailed off, highly displeased.

"Damn," Nick said. "I didn't handle that well."

"No, you didn't." Santana stared out at the Range Ranger, privately sympathizing with Nick. What Nick didn't realize was that getting his car fixed in a town this small wasn't going to be easy.

"I'm going to see if they took my dress!" Sierra turned to fly out the door, but Emma stopped her.

"You stay inside. Go sit back down. I'll check." She looked at Santana. "Make her go back to the table."

Nick turned instantly, taking Sierra's arm and guiding her back to her chair. Santana followed, surprised when his sister wound her arm through Nick's.

That was a very bad sign. If Sierra was feeling better, she'd be more likely to kick Nick than lean on him. He followed Emma out the door, unwilling to let her out of his sight while there were hoodlums around.

"Maybe we should phone the captain and ask him to send someone to pick us up. A taxi would be expensive. I think Sierra needs to get home," Emma said when he reached her.

He peered through the windows of the dark vehicle.

"She'll be happy to know no one wants the stupid dress except her."

Emma shook her head. "Sierra's proud of that stupid dress, as you call it, and Nick seems happy to be in on her dream, right?"

Santana was too worried about his sister to care about irrational pipe dreams. "Let's get you back inside where it's warm in case whatever made Sierra ill is contagious."

"Kiss me first," Emma said, to his surprise. He complied instantly, tugging her to him by her coat lapels, sinking his mouth against hers. She moaned, moving closer, and suddenly, the rapid snowfall and below-freezing chill no longer bothered Santana.

"You have me absolutely mesmerized, Dr. Glass."

"With one kiss?"

"It's more than that." He kissed her again, holding her, loving the feel of her in his arms. Her mouth was soft and sweet under his, allowing him entrance.

"Quit worrying." She stood on her tiptoes, drawing his head down for one last lingering kiss. "I'm never sick."

"Just like my sister," he said, but she laughed at him and pulled him inside to the table where Nick and Sierra were engaged in a pie-sharing moment.

Santana tried not to notice that his sister seemed to be acting completely unlike herself as she and Nick stabbed at one slice of pie, downing it without conversation.

"This is good," Nick said, sounding surprised. "Ever had French silk pie? Miss Sugar brought us a piece on the house. Because of the tires and all the inconvenience," he said, his eyes twinkling.

"It was a make-up gift," Sierra explained. "Since Nick

snapped her head off. Additionally, she's offered us the use of two rooms in her bed and breakfast behind the tearoom."

"We're not staying," Santana said, "Nick can stay here and tend to his problem. You're going home to bed. We've got Joe to think about, and Emma's got a pet collection at her place."

"Don't fuss about me, brother," Sierra said. "Don't make any special plans because of me. I'm feeling better, thanks to either whatever she puts in this remedy bottle of hers, or what she puts in her pie. Best pie ever!"

He glanced at the window, seeing the snow falling faster, almost on cue.

"We could probably rent a truck from someone in this town," Santana said thoughtfully, "or a vehicle of some kind. Something to get us home."

"You should," Nick agreed. "Don't stay here because of me. Definitely get Sierra home to bed. Excuse me, I'm going to take some photos before the snow covers my car, and call my insurance company."

Nick retreated with his cell phone. "What has gotten into you?" Santana asked Sierra.

"Nothing." She looked at Emma. "You might call Jenny and ask her if she can go stay at your place to pet sit. Maybe she could even swing by and get Joe, if you think she could manage all of them." His sister's eyes had dark circles under them from the fever, but she certainly seemed to be feeling better. Santana had never seen pie cure a fever, and he didn't believe in magic potions, or remedies—whatever "Miss Sugar" had put in the bottle—but something seemed to have worked.

"We can give her the code to the house and tell her

where we have an open window, if she doesn't mind getting Joe," Sierra said to Santana.

"Do you really think we'll have to stay the night?" Emma asked as they sat back down.

"Unfortunately, the thieves stripped the whole thing. Basically, they left only the axles."

"Surely this town has a garage of some sort," Emma said, and Santana shrugged.

"Let's hope."

CHAPTER TEN

"We might as well get cozy so you can rest," Miss Sugar said, returning to the table after about half an hour had passed. "I don't see any way you're leaving town, to be honest."

Emma was thrilled the woman had convenient accommodations. She'd called Jenny, and Jenny had been delighted to run by and get Joe, then bunk over at Emma's with the pets, especially since Emma had just stocked the fridge. Jenny would have done the favor anyway, but the lure of food had definitely gotten a yelp of excitement out of her friend.

"Thank you for letting us stay with you." Emma followed Sierra, who Miss Sugar had definitely taken a shine to. The men had stayed back to discuss the car angle. Nick was clearly out of sorts, though resigned, to the fact that his vehicle wouldn't have driving ability for a couple of days. Santana was worried about his sister, though he tried to act relaxed. He kept glancing at the big plate glass windows, and Emma knew he was worried about the snowstorm. It really was coming down hard now, and Miss Sugar had cheerfully informed them that there was ice reported under the snow.

Jesus, Nick had muttered under his breath, and Emma had smiled in sympathy. He was so out of his element that it would be funny if Sierra weren't ill.

Although Sierra seemed to be making a rapid recovery. She had color back in her face, and the dark circles under her eyes had lost the bruised look.

"Here we go!" Miss Sugar guided them to a couple of stuffed chairs in front of a nice gas-lit fireplace. "You sit there, angel." She made sure Sierra was comfortable in front of the fire, and sat down across from them on a small sofa. "Well, sit," she told Emma. "We might as well wait for your men to decide what they're going to do."

They knew what they had to do. They were just fighting it. It wasn't in Nick's or Santana's natures to accept roadblocks. Nick was a man used to being able to buy what he needed in life, and Santana used his muscles and determination to solve his issues.

In this case, they were defeated by a trifecta of strange occurrences. She took the chair Miss Sugar indicated, glad to be near a fire.

"Thank you for the remedy. I feel much better."

"Homeopathy," their hostess said with conviction. "I've found it very useful over the years. You just had a little something bugging you. Fortunately, I had the right remedy on hand!"

Emma didn't know if she believed in remedies, but even if it was just a placebo effect, she was thankful for it.

"Now let's see," Miss Sugar said, "I'm trying to remember

what I know about Star Canyon. There was that fire there recently, of course. Terrible tragedy."

Emma stiffened, not able to look at Sierra.

"Yes," Sierra murmured.

"Melly Shelby was so upset. She said her cousin Mary was just devastated. They say there was an accelerant used in that fire. I can never figure out why people do such things. But then, I don't understand why we've been hit by tire thieves." She shook her head. "They say they come in from the big city, and work a small town over. Anybody who is parked on the street is fair game. But in broad daylight!"

Sierra leaned forward. "Who said an accelerant was used in the fire?"

"Well, it's common knowledge," Miss Sugar said. Emma glanced at Sierra, alarmed. It wasn't common knowledge in Star Canyon—at least not in their close-knit group. And Captain Martin would have told them. He would have let Sierra and Santana know if there'd been any developments.

"Oh, it was definitely set on purpose. And it all had to do with that fire starter in Star Canyon," Miss Sugar rambled on.

"Fire starter?" Emma asked.

"A firebug. They said there's been a rash of small fires, but the one that took that poor fire captain's life was the biggest. Such a shame. They said he was such a good man. Excuse me, I'll see if the gentlemen need anything. Only way I know to keep men from being more upset than they already are is good food. Or at least it works around here."

She strode off. Emma looked at Sierra.

"Why didn't you tell her it was your father?"

"I don't know," Sierra stared off into space before

taking a deep breath. "But I just learned more than I ever knew before. I wonder if Santana knows."

"I doubt it. He would have told you."

Sierra nodded. "He would have. That leaves me to wonder why Captain Martin hasn't told us that he has more information."

"You realize Miss Sugar is a gossip, in spite of her good intentions. And you know how small towns are, word travels fast that isn't always true."

Sierra rubbed her hands over her arms. "What do you think about Nick?"

"Nothing much. He's nice. Seems genuine." Emma looked at her friend. "It's hard for me to trust anyone new to town. Everyone that I know, I've known all my life."

Miss Sugar came back inside. "Well, let me get you to your rooms. Range Rover Man has decided to sleep inside his car, to keep it from further damage. His friend says he's going to sit in here for a while, but that you two are to take the rooms." Miss Sugar smiled. "I get the feeling they're going to take turns keeping watch over the car."

"I suppose that's best." Emma stood. "Thank you for letting us stay, Miss Sugar."

"Mr. Range Rover paid me up front, and thankfully, I've got comfortable rooms available. The snow is really piling up outside, but you'll be warm in here. And I've got to dig out a blanket or two to give that young fellow. He doesn't look like the type who's done much bunking behind the wheel."

Emma smiled. "I'm positive you're right."

They followed the friendly proprietress down the hall. "Each of these rooms has their own bath. I think you'll find everything you need. If you want breakfast, it's served at seven a.m. sharp. How are you feeling?" she asked Sierra.

"I can't believe it, but I think you fixed me right up."

Miss Sugar nodded. "Homeopathy's great stuff. Goodnight, ladies."

Emma stared after Miss Sugar as she trundled back down the hall with her purposeful gait. "I'm going to call and check on Jenny. If you start feeling ill again, let me know."

"Thanks for everything, Emma." She went into the room on the left side of the hall. "I didn't mean to involve you in my adventures. But I'm glad you're here."

Emma smiled. "I wouldn't have missed it. Get some sleep."

Sierra closed her door, and Emma put her backpack on the bed in her room. She called and checked on Jenny, made sure all was well at the clinic, then closed her door quietly and went down the hall. She wasn't sure what she was looking for, but something told her Miss Sugar wasn't done talking.

There was always more to learn from a gregarious soul like Miss Sugar.

She found her in the café, wiping down the tables. "Can I help?"

"Mercy, no. You go on to bed." Miss Sugar smiled at her. "I've run this café and bed and breakfast for thirty years. Cleaning the tables at night and tidying up is how I get myself wound down for the next day."

Emma thought that might be true—but then again, the Range Rover could be seen from just about any angle, and Emma had the strangest sensation Miss Sugar was more interested in that than in the tidiness of her café. Though to be fair, her food was good, and her tearoom very clean. But she kept glancing surreptitiously toward the window, and Emma felt certain it wasn't just the snow that had her attention.

Emma picked up a local newspaper—really more of a brochure, two sheets of rather plain black-on-white text—and sat down to read.

"If you're looking for the big fellow, he said he was leaving to find some trouble."

Emma looked up. Assuming Miss Sugar was speaking of Santana, she said, "He's not in the car with Nick?"

"Nope. That young fellow's got to be cold. The snow is four inches thick on the top of his car. There's ice underneath everything. Quite a snowfall, I'd say."

"What kind of trouble can anybody find in a snowstorm? Isn't everything closed for the night?"

"I mentioned that there was always a darts game across the way in Peter Miller's barber shop. Your friend said he'd check it out." Miss Sugar smiled. "Of course, there's also a beer to be found."

Emma was surprised that Santana would leave Sierra to play darts. "I think I'll check on Nick."

"Oh, I've been keeping an eye on him. Every now and again, he switches on the car. Probably to charge his phone." Miss Sugar went in the kitchen, returning with a Styrofoam cup of coffee and a plastic baggie with cookies in it. "Don't fall down out there. I don't want to be sued for the limb you'd no doubt break in this weather. Tell him breakfast is at seven a.m. sharp."

"I will. Thank you." She took the food and went outside, heading to the driver's side. As she'd suspected, the window was iced up. After a few shoves, Nick managed to get the door open. He took the coffee gratefully, and the cookie bag.

"Thanks."

"No problem. Where's Santana?"

"I'm not my cousin's keeper."

She glanced across at Peter Miller's. "I'm going to join you for a minute."

"Good luck getting the door open."

"I work with large animals. I'll see if I've got brute strength enough to crack it open. I hate to see you suffering out here alone."

She went around to the passenger side, relieved to find that door not as caked with ice. She got in, not surprised that Nick had his car charger plugged in.

"Getting a lot of work done?"

"Surprisingly, yes. California's two hours behind, so that helps. And London is several hours ahead. Life's good, despite the storm."

"And the lack of wheels."

"Now that part sucks." Nick drank his coffee. "I think Santana went to see if the locals know anything about tire thieves around here."

She stiffened. "He didn't go to play darts?"

"Well, he might do that. But his parting words to me were *I'm going to check out the local grapevine and experts on wheel removal.*"

Emma didn't like the sound of that. "Miss Sugar says the thieves come from the city."

"Santana said Miss Sugar might be covering her ass."

Emma considered it. "It's possible."

"Sure. No one wants to taint their town. It's bad for

business. And civic pride is important in small towns, anyway. How's Sierra?"

"She seems much better. Miraculously cured." Emma wouldn't have believed it if she hadn't seen it.

"That was smoke and mirrors for your benefit. Whatever was bugging Sierra disappeared just as fast as it came," Nick scoffed. "Her cure had nothing to do with that bottle of water she drank."

That was probably true. "I think I'll go check on him."

Nick glanced at her. "I doubt he'd approve."

"Why?"

"Because he just wouldn't. You know that. Santana doesn't even like me sitting in this car. That's why he's appointed himself guardian of the misfits."

"Misfits?"

Nick shrugged. "You think he's happy about being stuck in a small town in a snowstorm with a man who took over his home and his livelihood, his somewhat rebellious little sister, and his veterinarian girlfriend? With missing wheels and a too-friendly B&B owner, and a vintage—putting it kindly—wedding gown in the backseat? This is a Navy SEAL nightmare."

"For the record, I'm not the girlfriend." She got out of the car. "Don't freeze to death."

Nick shrugged. "I'm learning survival skills, and Miss Sugar assures me that these are wool blankets. She swears I'll be warm as toast."

She got out of the car. "Glad to hear it."

"Emma."

"Yes?" She leaned down to look in the car at him.

"Just go back inside. Santana will yell my ear off if he finds out you left."

"I'll be back in five minutes. Tops."

He tapped his Rolex. "Don't make me get out of these blankets to come after you."

Emma smiled. "You won't have to."

She closed the door and carefully negotiated her way across the street. The shop was dark inside, but when she pushed the door, it swung open, a bell tinkling on the handle. "Hello?"

Raucous laughter and the sounds of male camaraderie erupted from somewhere in the back of the barber shop. She went in the direction of the noise and found a door marked Employees Only.

Maybe twenty men were inside, engrossed in a soccer game on a huge TV, neglecting the six dart boards on an opposite wall. In the thick of the scrum was Santana, leaning against a bar, staring at the screen, drinking a beer. A goal was scored, a yell went up, and high fives were passed all around.

Emma quietly crept out, relieved that he was having a good time. Very likely for the first time since he'd returned home, he'd found a place where he could relax and unwind from deployment, from everything that had happened since he'd come back.

She rapped on the window as she went by Nick's car and opened the door. "You're missing a great time over there."

He looked surprised. "At this time of night, in this town?"

"Don't be such a snob. Go have a beer. They've got a big screen TV that would probably impress even you."

Emma smiled and shut the door. "Goodnight, Miss

Sugar," she called, and Miss Sugar's head popped around the corner from the kitchen.

"Good night! Seven a.m. sharp, earlier if you'd like! Tell your crew!"

She'd forgotten to mention it to Nick, and Santana didn't care about breakfast right now. There was time for that later. She went down the hall and out the door that separated the establishments, crossing the small stone pathway. Inside the bungalow, she listened at Sierra's door.

Hearing nothing, Emma went into her room, took a fast shower in the cramped but clean bathroom, and hopped in bed, grateful for the clean sheets and the wool blanket on the bed.

Miss Sugar was right: her blankets were warm as toast.

• • •

Emma was just about to fall asleep—her eyelids were so heavy she was two seconds from the best sleep she'd had in years—no dogs, no pets to worry about, this was like being on vacation—when she heard her bedroom door open.

She froze, her eyes snapping open. She was positive she'd locked the door. "Who's there?"

The door closed. Emma blinked. Maybe she'd heard the door across the hall opening. But there'd been a slight shaft of light peeking through the darkness for just a second before the door shut.

She squealed as something large fell across her bed.

CHAPTER ELEVEN

"Sorry," Santana said. "That wasn't the most romantic entrance I've ever made."

She sat up, relieved. "What are you doing?"

"Checking on you."

"Did you hurt yourself? What did you just trip over?"

"I think your boots. Or my own big feet."

Emma smiled in the darkness. "Are you under the influence?"

He snorted. "Not from three beers."

"I wasn't expecting company."

"Obviously, considering you left a booby trap between the bed and the door for me to kill myself on. And yet, I should be used to evading dogs and cats and parakeets."

"Lovebirds. My beautiful birds are lovebirds." She heard boots thudding to the floor. "Again, why are you in my room?" Emma asked.

"You checked on me over at the local excuse for male entertainment. Thought you might need me."

"No, you didn't. You thought I was spying. Probably sent by your sister, that's what you thought."

He crawled into bed, flopping onto the pillow, sighing with what sounded like exhaustion. She realized he'd probably been up since four a.m. with the cattle at the ranch, before he'd decided to drive Nick to the airport.

Before their adventure had ever begun.

"All right, I didn't think you needed me. But I was pretty sure I needed you."

A warm glow started inside her. "Is Nick still outside?"

"Do you really think that money-obsessed carpetbagger is going to let anything else happen to his beloved heap?"

She smiled in the darkness. "Now that you put it that way, I guess not."

"That's right. If I've learned anything about my unexpected cousin-on-paper-only, it's that he respects money more than anything else in the world."

"I don't think he's all that mercenary."

"Don't rob me of my delusions. I need them."

"Oh." It was important to keep separation between he and Nick so he wouldn't resent him. As long as Santana was the employee, and Nick the employer, Santana didn't have to think: He could just work. For however long that relationship remained beneficial.

It was good for both of them.

"So who won the game?"

"I have no idea." He sighed, sounding sleepy. "I went looking for information, and found a whole world I never knew existed. Back room bar and shenanigans. My brothers would love that place."

"You miss them, don't you?"

"I miss our family—the way it was. Yeah. I miss what we were. Before."

Emma leaned against the pillow, tucking the sheet under her arms. "I'm so sorry."

"It's nobody's fault. Except maybe dad's. But what the hell. Gambling's a terrible addiction, and I'm glad he was able to break it, at least to some extent." He sighed again, deeply.

Emma thought it best to change the subject. "When does Nick think they can bring him new wheels and tires?"

"The boys across the way think they've got a set of wheels they can temporarily put on, at least so a tow truck can load him up and take his precious hunk of junk to the city for extra-special treatment at whatever fairy tale store is required for rich folks and their expensive rides. How's Sierra?"

"Last I saw, much improved." Emma's brows furrowed. "It was so weird how that fever hit her. My guess is that it was around one hundred two."

"She was definitely ill." He was quiet for a minute. "She's not herself anymore. The truth is, she's been acting strange ever since we found out about our father."

Emma thought about Miss Sugar's astonishing gossip. "She doesn't talk about it much." Actually, Sierra was more quiet than her brothers about her grief. "I'd like to say that Sierra is just being quiet, but in some ways, she was the wild one of your family, I'd have to admit. I get why you're worried, but maybe it'll pass in time, Santana."

"It's the tattoos and the hair that worry me. She was never really a renegade."

"I wouldn't take those things necessarily as the mark of

a renegade. You have a tattoo." He had a pretty spectacular lightning strike on his upper back, right shoulder.

"It's the piercings and everything else." Santana shifted on the bed. "It's the wedding dress store, too."

"Why is that cause for alarm?"

"It just worries me how fast she jumped into an arrangement with Nick."

"You did."

"Yeah. But this magic wedding dress business is crazy. Sierra knows nothing about owning a store, nothing about retail. I don't like any of it. But there's not much I can do about it."

"She has to give it a shot. If it doesn't work out, she'll go to work at the fire station," she reminded him.

"Over my cold, dead body."

Santana went silent for a moment, then she felt his big frame leave the bed. By the sudden tugging, she could tell he was pulling his boots back on. "Where are you going?"

"You need your rest. I'll see you in the morning. Miss Sugar says seven a.m. sharp for breakfast, or we go hungry. Goodnight, Emma."

He left, closing the door quietly behind him, and Emma knew sleep was going to be impossible now that he'd left her without even a kiss.

* * *

Nick started when the passenger-side door opened again. When had his car become the local hangout?

Sierra got in, slamming his door with a bit more force than a car this expensive required. "Careful," he chided.

"This is just a car," Sierra glared at him. "Nothing special. It's metal and glass and some really nice leather seats." She reclined her chair.

Nick wasn't certain how he felt about that. He already had a wedding dress taking up space in the back, where technically he could at least lie down if he moved the damn thing. He was probably more comfortable up here, though. "Do you have a point?"

"Yes. It's that you shouldn't worship things so much that you freeze your balls off."

"Says the woman with an ancient, moth-eaten gown in my back seat." What had happened to him? The bachelor lifestyle was one he'd savored, enjoying it to the fullest.

Until everything had changed.

Damn Dad, anyway. Why did you have to leave me with these five responsibilities?

Of course the Darks weren't his responsibility, technically. He could just walk away.

"It's not moth-eaten!" Sierra shot him yet another glare, which would probably look really menacing on anyone but her. She had the cutest pixie face and expressive eyes, and darling full lips.

She also had face jewelry and wild hair that looked like she'd stuck a finger in a socket. And a sassy mouth.

He shifted in the seat, thinking he was in no danger at all of his balls being frozen. Something about Sierra had the strangest ability to heat him right up, to an uncomfortable degree.

"This dress is a piece of history of a bygone era," Sierra told him.

"Are we opening a museum or a dress shop?"

"I am opening a place where dreams come true."

"And I'm financing this."

"Yes, out of the corner of your Scrooge-like heart that has some desire for excitement and human contact left in it. Give me a corner of that blanket."

He tossed half of both of the blankets over her, feeling weirdly like two kids making a fort out of the family linen. It was an experience he'd never had, lacking siblings. Nick glanced at his uninvited guest, noting Sierra's eyes were closed, her hands fisted in the blankets, holding them close to her chin.

"You shouldn't be out here," he said gruffly. "You just got over a fever. We hope."

"Miss Sugar's spoonful of sugar worked. I'm fine."

"You're not that susceptible."

"Look. For years all we had out in Star Canyon was a D.O. We lived on home remedies. Not everybody needs to run to a fancy doctor with a prescription pad every time they fart."

"Are you suggesting I do?"

"Fart?" She shrugged. "Everybody does. Except I forget, you're not Mr. Everybody. You're special."

He sighed. "Why are you out here, heating up the inside of my car?"

"Because you need company. Being lonely is boring."

"You think I'm boring?"

She rolled her head to look at him. "Don't you think you're boring?"

It just so happened that he did, but he wasn't going to admit it. "So you came out here to tell me I'm a selfish stiff who's so Ebenezer Scrooge I won't get out of my costly chariot, and if I so much as sneeze, I'd feel the need to dial up my premium physician for an instant consultation."

"Sorry," she said, "it was too much to dump on you at once, wasn't it? And anyway, that's not why I'm here. But I'm crabby, so try to overlook it."

"Thank you," he said mildly.

"You can sleep in my room with me," Sierra said.

"I…beg your pardon?" Nick was dumbfounded.

"There's no reason to be out in this Arctic tomb. You can sleep in bed with me. I promise not to touch you."

She sounded as if that was the last thing she'd ever want to do, akin to handling a large snake.

"I think Miss Sugar would be offended."

"Miss Sugar may have to deal with it."

He considered Sierra's pointed look. She definitely meant what she was saying. "This is a trap, right?"

"What?" She raised a brow. "You mean the kind of trap where I invite you to sleep in my room, then claim I'm having your baby? Don't be stupid. My brothers would kill you if they even thought you touched me."

"Do they do that often?"

"Threaten suitors?" Sierra laughed. "My brothers are well understood in Star Canyon. They don't have to threaten anyone. You, they'd kill."

He straightened. "So you're inviting me to walk into a dangerous situation."

"Thrilling, isn't it?"

"Not really." He burrowed down further in his seat. "I prefer females who are less encumbered by marauding brothers."

"Yeah, well. You and every other man." She sighed. "I was hoping you were different."

He looked at her. "Why?"

"Men with courage are hard to find."

"Courage? Dealing with homicidal cousins would make me a courageous figure to you?"

"We're not really cousins, you know."

"It might be better if we were."

"That's...weird, even coming from the world's biggest pinhead."

She didn't understand that filial distance was a good thing. How could he want to kiss Sierra as much as he did?

"Anyway," Sierra said, "back to my homicidal brothers, I've got one at the ranch taking care of your herd. Hope you don't mind."

He glanced at her, stunned. "Which brother?"

"Actually, all three of them. Luke, Cisco, and Romero. Although I don't think Cisco will hang around long."

"Santana didn't mention this."

"He doesn't know." She met his gaze with piercing eyes. "And until I figure out how to tell him, you're not going to tell him, either."

"Why can't you just tell him? They're grown men. No need to hide."

"They came back to work for you."

His brows rose. "Instead of going to find their destinies on some remote island or desert, they've decided to return and work the family ranch that's no longer theirs?"

"That's it."

"Why did they tell you instead of Santana?"

"I asked them to come back, just for a couple of

months. It's going to be Christmas soon. We need to be together during the holidays. It's normal for families. Didn't you know?"

"So your brothers are running the ranch for me right now?"

"I told them you needed the help. We're stranded here for who knows how long."

"Tomorrow."

"Well, ranch life doesn't wait until you show back up in your Jaguar."

"Range Rover."

"Doesn't matter."

"Thank you for sending them over," he said, thinking he now had four brothers to get through if he was ever going to—

To what? Kiss this wild woman? Date her? They were so different from each other he shouldn't even be thinking what he was thinking. Not about her soft lips, her big eyes, her delicate body, the sparks she threw off when she lit up with her harebrained schemes—

"That's good. Nice to know. And your secret's safe with me. Although it won't be a secret much longer, once we get back. Now get out."

Sierra looked at him. "What?"

"Get out of my car. Please." Nick really, really wanted her to go. If she didn't, he couldn't be held responsible for not tasting those lips.

He'd be royally screwed if he did.

"Why?" Sierra demanded.

"Because you're bothering me. I'm trying to work. It's the first time since I've met you Darks that I've actually had utter silence. No barking dogs, no scrawny tie-dye-haired woman sassing me, no wedding gown ridiculousness—"

She gasped. "You don't mean that!"

"Out of the car. Time is money, and you're taking up time I could be working."

"It's all about money for you, isn't it?"

"Yes, it is. Goodnight."

She got out, peering back in at him for a second. "If you get tired of being a frozen freak, there's space for you in my room."

It was so tempting he wondered if he was stupid to pass it up. "Your brother would take a chunk out of my hide."

"Don't be a boring chickenshit, Nick Marshall."

No one in any boardroom would have ever called him such. "We discussed your homicidal brothers, didn't we?"

"For the record, my room has two beds. I wasn't seducing you, dork."

She slammed the door, drawing a wince from him. His car had never been treated with anything but the softest touch. Then again, what did it matter? The thieves had left his car axles perched on cinder blocks, a well-practiced maneuver to get wheels on and off with a minimum of fuss. She was right: the car was just metal and glass.

She was beauty and sass.

He wasn't going to tell her the truth about her birth parent records. That job he'd assigned to her brother, his foreman.

I'm an asshole like my father.

He told himself Sierra really did have homicidal brothers, but that wasn't why he needed distance.

She might not have been attempting to seduce him, but

if he went into her room, he damn sure would be hard-pressed not to seduce her.

He'd keep her secret, though. Just like he was keeping his.

He settled back down in the seat, and told himself to go to sleep. The door opened again, but he didn't open his eyes. Damn it, had these people never heard of texting? They could reach him faster that way, and with a whole lot less bother to him.

"If you get out," a raspy voice said, "we can fix up your car and get you at least to the nearest town."

He jumped. The man looked perfectly fine, in an overgrown, flannel-wearing sort of way. "I have a service coming tomorrow, thanks. Do I know you?"

"I'm Miss Sugar's brother."

"Ah." Nick got out of the car reluctantly, and the man closed the passenger-side door. Nick glanced at the truck the man drove. There was a stack of tires haphazardly thrown in the back, very visible thanks to the spotlight on the top of the man's truck emitting enough light to blind angels. "Are those my tires?"

"Could be. I just buy them when they come my way."

Nick approached the truck bed. Those *were* his tires, high-quality, expensive tires that weren't anything like the stacks of tires beneath. Great, just great. He was the victim of a scam, and Miss Sugar was the chief con artist. "You're Miss Sugar's brother, you say?"

"I am. Name's Sid."

"What's going on?" Santana asked, coming out of the diner. "That light on your truck is shining through the whole damn—are those your tires, Nick?"

"Yes. He apparently doesn't have my wheels, though."

"Doug Weathers probably has those," Sid informed them. "He buys 'em, no questions asked."

"He doesn't want them," Santana said, stunning Nick. "I ought to report this establishment for preying on its customers."

"Hey!" Sid drew his girth up. "I didn't know these were his tires!"

"Hit the road, or I'm calling the law."

"Sheriff's my cousin!" Sid exclaimed.

"Then I'll call the Better Business Bureau and a few other places. News stations, for one," Santana said. "Go."

"Try to do a man a good deed, and this is how I get treated," Sid said. "Fine. Sit out here and freeze your stupid citified carcass."

He drove off, highly indignant. Nick looked at Santana. "Is there a reason I didn't want my tires back?"

"Wait for it," Santana said, and Nick was surprised to see Sid stop his truck in the middle of the icy street. He got out, hustled to the truck gate. Opening it, he tossed the four tires Nick had claimed were his into the street.

"I don't want any trouble," Sid called to them. "And I'd appreciate it if you don't mention this to my sister!"

He got in his truck and drove off.

"Wow. Did you know he would do that?"

"I knew sense would eventually kick into his meaty brain. Let's go in and get some coffee. Miss Sugar's just set some out fresh, which I was coming to tell you when I saw you had company."

Nick wondered if Santana knew that Sid wasn't the only company he'd had. They tossed the tires into the back of the Range Rover and went inside Miss Sugar's.

She had coffee and fresh biscuits on a table for them. "Hope you slept well!"

"Thank you, Miss Sugar." Nick shook his head and sat across from Santana, who seemed unconcerned about anything but hot coffee. "The ways of small towns elude me just a bit."

"You think?" Santana asked drily.

"You'd be just as awkward in my world."

"More." Santana bit into a biscuit. "I wouldn't even try to fit where you come from."

Nick wondered why he was bothering to try to fit into the Darks' world. Frankly, small town life probably wasn't going to work out for him. Thanks to the internet and cell phones and good roads, he could run just as much of his business from Star Canyon as he would normally—outside of the lunch and dinner meetings. But he didn't have to do those to make business happen. He'd just done them out of a sense of…loneliness.

"So, just a word of caution," Santana said. "I wouldn't let my sister talk you into anything else."

Nick's gaze shot to meet Santana's. He wondered if he had guilty stamped on his forehead. "Like?"

"Running for town council."

Nick laughed. "No, really."

Santana shrugged. "She will. Or something else civic-minded."

"I don't have time."

"You have nothing but time. And you'll want to make her happy. Everybody always does. Sierra has that effect on people."

Nick looked at him warily. "I'm a committed bachelor."

Santana laughed. "Join the crowd."

"No, I really am. I know you and Emma are, um, close."
He hesitated at the quick glower on Santana's face. "But I'm
not interested in Sierra, not like that. We're like sand and
water, we'd mix and make a soggy mess."

Santana looked at him. "All I said was everybody wants
to make Sierra happy. How did this get to be about you and
Sierra hanging out on beaches?"

Nick sipped his coffee. "Just making sure what we're
talking about."

Santana's face was practically stone, looking very much
like the homicidal maniac Sierra had mentioned. "You've
got a thing for my sister," he said, his tone stunned.

Nick held up a hand. "Absolutely not."

"You poor bastard. She's already got you under her
spell. Well, good luck with that."

Nick blinked. "I don't need luck."

"You will. Oh, you will."

But then Emma walked in, looking fresh as morning
sunshine. Nick noticed Santana change from stone man to a
man with a smile—however small—on his face, and thought
he wasn't the only poor bastard in Star Canyon.

Misery loved company, and there was plenty of that to
go around.

Emma sat down, and Santana poured her some coffee.
"Nick got his tires back."

"Really?" Emma looked at Nick. "No wheels, though?"

"Not yet," Santana said. "But I expect we'll have
everything we need in the next thirty minutes to get us back
to Star Canyon."

"I got a text from Jenny," Emma said. "She said there

was all kinds of snow dumped in Star Canyon. But since your brothers are home, one of them is running by to get Joe from her. It might have been Cisco."

Santana stilled in the act of biting a biscuit. He put it on his plate. "Why are my brothers at the ranch?"

Sierra joined them at the table, her hair standing straight up. Nick wondered how he could think a wild girl like this would ever fit in his world. She would stick out at cocktail parties. Other wives would stare at her. Eclectic didn't fare well in the world he lived in, not this kind of eclectic which was actually a polite way of saying eccentric.

"What?" Sierra asked Santana. "Why is your face frozen like you just bit into something gross?"

"Our brothers came back. They're at the ranch right now."

"I know." Sierra nodded. "I was going to tell you, but I found out last night. When I walked past the fireplace room, you were sacked out." She looked at Nick. "So, you're no good at keeping secrets."

"You knew?" Santana howled at Nick.

"Don't get me involved." Nick raised his hands. "I'm going to borrow Sierra's shower. See if you can work your magic and get my wheels back. I don't think I can hang around you Darks much longer. Jeez."

He stomped off, not about to get caught in the middle of a Dark family fracas.

Sierra followed him to her room, closing the door behind them.

"I didn't tell him. Emma did."

"I know. She just told me." Sierra looked at him, and

he wished desperately there wasn't a closed door separating them from the rest of their companions.

"Well, get out. I can't shower with you in here." He glanced around the room, seeing only one double bed. "Hey, you told me there were two beds in here."

She shrugged.

"Are you coming on to me? Because if you are, I want you to know I don't want you to," he said, digging deep for resistance.

"Just came in to get my purse." Her gaze was laughing as she picked it up and went out.

Nick went straight to the shower, turning it on cold.

* * *

Emma went straight home to relieve Jenny of pet sitting duties, glad to be away from Santana. What exactly had happened between them on that short journey?

She found her friend sobbing into a pillow on the sofa. "Jenny! What's wrong?"

"One of the lovebirds died!" Jenny wailed. "I'm a failure as a pet aunt!"

"Oh, Jenny." She hugged her friend. "Don't cry. You're upsetting Gus and Bean. And me. My birds are very old. They don't live forever, you know." She and her father had picked them out together for a birthday present for her the year after her mother had died. She'd been seventeen. The birds were a sweet reminder, but she had the clinic, and that was a permanent link to her family.

"Nothing's ever died on my watch! I had to take it out and put it in a little baggie, then wrap a dish towel around it, and put it in a shoe box. The ground's too cold to bury anything right now, and I didn't know if you'd want to do it yourself."

"Jenny, you're a wonderful pet aunt. Please don't cry." She got her friend a tissue as Gus and Bean flailed at their feet for attention. "Hello, fellows. Are you trying to make Aunt Jenny feel better?"

"They've been so good." Jenny sniffled into her tissue. "Even Princess has been good and cuddles with me all the time. She used to be sort of unimpressed with me, but we really bonded. I thought we were all doing so well! And I was eating you out of house and home, reading a little case law, and watching some old Alfred Hitchcock TV shows. And then—"

"Don't think about it anymore." Emma patted her friend's arm. "Jenny, there's no one I trust more with my animals than you."

"Thank you." Jenny sniffled again. "How was the trip?"

"Strange." Emma didn't know what to think about anything that had happened. "It's like we were on this really weird adventure to find an old dress, and wound up finding out a lot about each other instead. Maybe too much." And maybe too much about themselves. After their recent lovemaking, she felt certain she and Santana shouldn't be so awkward with each other. But he'd been totally remote after he'd left her room that night.

I'm not going to think about it. I can't guess what was on his mind. If he wants to talk, he can find me.

She got up. "I'm going to get some hot tea. I'm bringing you some, too. You're staying here for the night, okay? The roads aren't good at all."

"Thank you," Jenny said, still not cheered. She padded after Emma into the kitchen, and the dogs followed, not about to let Emma out of their sight. "Is the dress beautiful?"

"In an old-fashioned, sort of sad way." Emma smiled. "Yes, it's lovely. But the story that went along with it was sort of a testimony to love that never happened."

"Well, that won't happen to you. Santana's on the case." Jenny giggled, and Emma was glad to see her smile, even if her opinion wasn't close to being right.

"Cisco, Romero, and Luke came back."

"What?" Jenny got up on a bar stool at the island, watching her set a kettle on. "Why?"

"What I've been able to learn from Sierra—who was so sick while we were gone that I'm not sure how much she actually knew and what she was making up—is that they took a crazy road trip. But they're back for the holidays."

Jenny's eyes went wide. She tossed the tissue into the trash. "Maybe they decided military life wasn't for them?" She sounded so hopeful.

"I don't know that they decided that, exactly." She set two teacups between them. "My guess is that they've decided to wait until after Christmas to make big decisions."

"You know," Jenny said, her voice soft, "I've always had kind of a thing for Cisc—"

Knocking on the door startled them. "I'll get it," Jenny said, sliding off the stool. Gus and Bean went nuts barking, so Emma couldn't hear who it was, but her heart leaped inside her. Maybe Santana had come by with Joe, and maybe those strange moments between them were nothing more than worry over Sierra.

She was stunned when Nick walked into the kitchen, followed by Santana. Her gaze met Santana's, surprised.

"Jenny, this is Nick Marshall. Nick, one of my dearest friends, Jenny Wright. Have a seat, please, everybody. Would you like some hot tea?"

To her surprise, Nick nodded. Santana moved his large frame onto a bar stool.

"If it's no trouble," he said courteously.

"It's not. What brings you two out? Last I saw you, you were heading to check on your new hands, Nick." Emma got out more tea bags and a couple of mugs for the guys, pulling the kettle off the stove once it started to rumble.

"Sierra left," Santana said, and Jenny and Emma both fastened their gazes on him.

"Left?" Emma asked.

"Town. We were wondering if she'd mentioned anything to you." Santana watched her as she poured tea for everyone.

"Not a word." She got out some cookies from Mary's bakery and put out dishes and napkins. "Why would she leave?"

"She said she could now. That she had the freedom to leave me and Nick to our own devices. That the ranch was in good hands."

Emma was dumbfounded. "What about the wedding store?"

"She left me with a leased space she's got practically ready for business." He sighed, staring down into his tea. "Not to mention the storeroom full of crap she's been stockpiling since the beginning of time."

Santana took a deep breath. "I realize she's in pain. I know everything's that's happened has hurt her. It's hurt all of us." He held up a hand. "Nick, this has nothing to do with you," he said, forestalling Nick's words, whatever he'd been about to say. "This isn't any easier on you," he told his cousin. "You've tried to be fair with us."

Jenny got up. "I'm going to take the pups outside, I think," she said softly. "They need a walk."

Gus and Bean were more than happy to joyously skitter out the door, all heaving tongues and scrambling paws. Emma sat on the counter. "I'm sorry I'm no help. The last person I ever thought would leave this town is Sierra. Especially with your brothers coming home. And Christmas so close."

"Their return gave her freedom." Nick stood. "I think I've overstayed my welcome in Star Canyon. So as much as I've enjoyed life in a small town, I think I'm going to return to what I know best."

They watched him walk out. Emma's gaze met Santana's.

"What the hell just happened?" Santana said.

"I'm not exactly certain, but it's possible your newfound cousin just ditched you."

CHAPTER TWELVE

Santana was stunned by Nick's abrupt exit from Emma's house. The man simply got up from the bar stool he'd been perched on and left. "Ditched? As in, left Star Canyon for good?"

"I think maybe in the short term, at least." Emma considered. "Something's bugging him."

"Yeah. What has gotten into everybody?" On paper, maybe it would seem best that Nick had gone. His arrival in their lives had certainly stirred up plenty of trouble.

Yet he hadn't wanted Nick to leave Star Canyon—or their lives. Their family tree had grown a strange branch, but it was a branch he hadn't envisioned losing.

He rubbed his face, scrubbing at his shadow, realizing he had no ride home. He didn't want Emma driving in the snow. One of his brothers could come get him. "What do you think he meant by overstayed his welcome?"

"I think just that he's ditching us, no hidden meaning," Emma said simply, and Santana realized she was right.

"He can't. He can't just up and leave Star Canyon. He has a ranch to run."

"Can you blame him? We're not an easy town to live in for outsiders."

"Blame him?" he echoed. "I don't blame him for anything." What was there to blame Nick for? He hadn't wanted them anymore than they'd wanted him.

"Back to Sierra, your sister mentioned that if the dress shop didn't work out, she was going to work at the fire station."

"No," Santana said automatically. "No, she's not."

No way was he losing his only sister the way he had their father. "No," he said again.

"You know why she feels that way," Emma said. "It's a part of your family. And Miss Sugar brought up the fire. I could tell it really got to Sierra, though she didn't say much about it. Now that I think about that, maybe it's no surprise Sierra feels like she needs some time to herself, Santana."

He couldn't bear to think about it. Jenny blew in on a puff of cold air and two rambling, delighted dogs following her every step, until they remembered their water bowl. They descended on it, sloshing water over the sides in their enthusiasm.

"They're getting better on the leash," Jenny announced. "But they're going to need a lot more work. And on that note, I'm going to make myself at home with a shower."

Jenny went off, still looking a bit glum.

"What's with her?" Santana asked.

Emma shook her head. "One of my lovebirds died while we were gone. It's upset her. She feels as if she's let me down."

"Jenny's pretty levelheaded. She knows nothing lasts forever." He glanced toward the birdcage, seeing the lone bird. "She's got a soft heart, though. Just like you."

"I'm a vet, Santana, I know how fortunate I was to have my birds as long as I did."

"Can I buy you another? No reason for a lovebird to be single. Kind of defeats the purpose of being a lovebird, I suppose."

She smiled. "I'd like that."

He felt something in his chest move, his heart giving him a strong kick, recognized that he was staring at the one thing that made him smile. "Have I ever told you how much I like your smile?"

Her eyes searched his, and it was like someone punched him. "I mean it. And I really like the way you listen. I know you hear me, and you don't try to cheer me up, or give me false words of encouragement. You're calm and steady, while everything else in my world right now is kind of a clusterfuck. FUBAR. Fucked up beyond all recognition."

"I don't know that I'm the port in the storm that you need, but I want to be here for you if you need me."

How could he tell her everything he felt? "I'm sorry for going radio silent before. I can't explain it."

"I don't need you to."

She looked at him with those clear, beautiful eyes, and Santana knew she meant every word. "I'm not taking you for granted. That's all I want you to know."

"I know," she said softly. "It's okay. Clusterfuck and all."

He smiled. "I'm going to call Cisco."

She nodded. "I need to check that Jenny found towels

and everything she needs, and make sure the dogs aren't in the shower with her. They really like water."

He watched her leave the room, her fanny swaying in her jeans. His mouth dried out, his gaze never leaving her. What was he doing? She was the opposite of him and his unique clan. Why wasn't he locking her down?

• • •

"Why did you come back?" Santana asked his brothers after Cisco had picked him up and brought him home. "Why did you leave in the first place?"

Romero, Cisco, and Luke looked at him, studying him from various perches in the rental house. It was going to be cramped with the four of them here, but he still wished Sierra hadn't left. She brought cheer and constant excitement, the kick in the pants they'd always needed.

Without her, the four of them weren't exactly going to be a barrel of laughs.

"We left," Cisco said, "because we were on a mission. We needed space and separation. Until we found out from Sierra that things weren't exactly under control around here. Then we decided to return."

"But just until after Christmas." Romero had a cap mashed down on his bald head—why had his brother shaved his head? Santana wondered. He looked like a serious grapefruit. "Then we're enlisting."

"All three of you?" Santana realized he'd be the only Dark left here. And Mr. Fancy Pants Nick had left. He should have known that a man with so many more worlds to conquer couldn't be satisfied in Star Canyon.

"You're a SEAL," Luke pointed out. "We're just following in your combat boots."

He couldn't keep them here. But it was going to suck without his family. "So, Christmas."

"Yeah." Romero nodded. "Tell Sierra to get her ass home. It'll be our last Christmas together for who knows how long."

Santana got up to get himself a longneck. He stared around the dim rental house, cataloguing the three bedrooms, two baths, peeling wallpaper in the small kitchen, the squeaky wooden floorboards, and the leaking shower. The house wasn't far from the Dark Ranch, but it felt like a world away. "Tell her yourself. Better yet, don't tell her at all." He peered into the rattling, ancient refrigerator that sounded like it was on its last few hours as a working appliance. "Sierra's having a few adjustment issues. Same as you did." He stood up, handing each of his brothers a beer. "It's cheap brew, but it fits the budget."

"What are you going to do?" Cisco asked. "What are we going to do?"

"Now that cousin Nick left us high and dry?" Santana shrugged. "Same thing I was. He can't just go off and desert his place. A city dude like him doesn't know that one just doesn't drive off and leave a working ranch. I'll get my paychecks out of him, no worries." He hadn't paid him yet, but he knew Nick would.

"He's going to have to make up his mind," Luke said. "He's either with us, or he'll sell the ranch."

"We don't want that," Romero said quietly. "With Nick owning it, we still have a connection to our home."

This was true, and maybe a shot to get it back. Somehow.

Work it off over several years? Nick was a businessman, money mattered to him—and everything had a price, right? Santana mused. "So the battle plan is to get Nick to return."

"And Sierra," Cisco said. "I'm not pleased with her at all."

"Oh, yeah? And where did you go during the two weeks you jaunted off?"

"Believe it or not," Cisco said, "we went down to Mexico."

"Mexico!" Santana glared at his brothers. "You took a vacation while everything was a mess here?"

"We went scuba diving in the Cenotes," Romero said, kicking back with his longneck. "And we enjoyed the local *cervezas* and *mujeres*."

Well, wasn't that a kick in the pants. The trouble with being the eldest was that the good sense the family possessed had gotten watered down with each child born. By the time the last kid arrived, clearly the Darks were out of the common sense gene.

But that wasn't possible. They shared no bloodline, no genes. Santana swallowed hard. "Part of the problem we're having is that Dad kept a lot of stuff from us. And I don't think he ever intended to tell us." No paperwork had been left behind, no letters, nothing. Just the documents with the lawyers. No wonder Sierra had gone a little bit off the deep end. "Shit," he muttered. "We need to figure this out."

"It's the same as it always was, Santana," Cisco said. "Different house, different story, maybe. But we're all the same. We're brothers."

Romero nodded. "Look, we don't have to go. We can

stay, help out with the ranch. If you need extra hands, we're here for you."

"And we can do some time at Star Canyon #1," Luke said. "Captain says he can use us."

"No," Santana said sharply.

His brothers stared at him.

"We've got enough to do at our own place." Santana got up, paced to the window. It was strange looking out at a front yard that wasn't his. He was used to a wide-open vista meeting his vision from any window at the Dark ranch. "If you stay, that is. And you don't have to."

"You can't do it on your own," Luke said. "And who knows how long it will be before Mr. Country Club decides he's not cut out for the working ranch life and decides to cut his losses?"

It was a plausible question. "All we can control is what happens on a day to day basis."

"You think Dad knew he was leaving behind one massively screwed-up mess for us?" Luke asked. "Was he just avoiding responsibility by not telling us himself?"

"That's what we just can't get past." Romero went and got four more longnecks from the fridge. "It just doesn't seem like Dad to be irresponsible."

And yet they hadn't really known Sonny Dark, had they? "It doesn't matter," Santana finally said. "Dad's decisions were his own. I'm sure he thought about his options with great care. He loved us. You all know that. And he was a good father. We lacked for nothing."

He said it for his own sake as much as his brothers'.

A knock on the door caught their attention. "Come in," Santana yelled. There was no need to stand on ceremony in a house that had fourteen hundred square feet to it. They were all of six feet from the door.

Captain Phil came in, lowering his head so he wouldn't hit the cheap light fixture hanging in the foyer.

"Hello, Captain." Santana got up to shake his hand, welcome him inside. Romero got him a longneck and they all settled onto the dingy sofas and chairs again. "What brings you out to see us?"

"Heard the boys were back." Phil nodded at his brothers. "If you're back for good, I've got a place for you at the station."

"Not yet," Santana said mildly, not acknowledging the flash of fear he felt every time the station was mentioned. Their father shouldn't have died. He was an experienced firefighter with many saves. Did he have to lose brothers, too?

"Sierra called me," Phil said, and Santana tried to remember what Emma had said about Sierra talking to Miss Sugar in Lightning Canyon. There'd been something, hadn't there?

"She have something on her mind?"

"Yeah. As a matter of fact, she did." Phil looked around at the four of them. "She said she and Joe are planning to be home the middle of January, most likely."

"Joe!" He sprang to his feet, looking around. Joe's food and water bowls were gone. His dog bed wasn't in the corner. Leash gone from the wall. "Damn it! She took my dog!"

Only it wasn't "his" dog. Sierra had gotten Joe for him on his return from deployment, saying he'd need the dog. And the dog needed him. But Joe had been Sierra's dog first.

"Sierra said you didn't have time to take care of him, not with everything you have to do. Said she needed him more than you do, and Emma agreed, apparently." Captain nodded. "When she returns, Sierra says she's going to firefighter school. She wants to join Star Canyon #1." Phil looked at Santana with great sympathy. "She said to tell you that her mind's made up, and to get all your fussing about it out of your system before she comes back because she doesn't want to hear your endless bellyaching. She says she got some fever recently, and she had a vision that changed her life. I didn't understand all that, but I got that she was serious as hell."

That flash of fear Santana had experienced earlier was a full-sized sledgehammer now crushing his heart.

CHAPTER THIRTEEN

"I'm leaving," Santana said suddenly. "You boys help yourselves to what's left of the beer. Thanks for coming by, Cap'n."

"Where are you going?" Cisco asked.

"Out. Carry on as usual." He jostled into a jacket.

"Carry on? The situation is SNAFU. That's why we're talking. We have to fix it," Cisco pointed out.

Santana smiled to himself at the acronym. Situation normal: all fucked up. Well, that was the new normal, and it wasn't going to change by chatting over a few beers. At least not today.

But he could fix something.

"I'll be back."

Santana headed out into the cold, got into his truck, already missing Joe's big furry body beside him, peering out the window. But he understood why Sierra had wanted Joe. She needed comfort, a connection—and God only knew she'd been the one anchor in the family for a long time.

He drove to Emma's, and pounded on the door.

She answered, her hair up in a white towel, a blue robe wrapped around her. Her toes were bare, toenails painted blue. He swallowed hard. "Hi."

Emma didn't reply. She merely looked at his face and opened the door wide.

She closed the door, looking at him, waiting for him to speak. He couldn't, his throat was closed up. His emotions were too near the surface.

She kissed him, and he lost it.

"I don't have anything to offer you."

"I didn't know you were supposed to be offering me something," Emma said, kissing him again. She slipped her hand along his side, just above his belt, and he couldn't hold back his wall of reservation any longer.

He took her lips, hard instantly at the moan he drew from her. He knew she was bare underneath the robe, and it drove him mad. Still, he craved the invitation he wanted to hear only from Emma, so he framed her face with his hands, kissing her urgently, trying to tell her how much she meant to him. That she had somehow, inexplicably, become his new anchor.

"Bed," Emma said, gasping against his mouth—and that was the invitation he'd been dying to hear. He scooped her into his arms, carrying her down the hall to her room. Miraculously the dogs didn't complain when he closed the door with a boot, never letting go of Emma. He couldn't get enough of her mouth. The freight train roaring through him was on fire.

"Bed," Emma said again, and it finally registered that

she wanted it hot and fast and sexy. She needed this as much as he did.

He lay her on the bed but she got up on her knees, undoing his shirt in a mad rush. He kissed her mouth, her neck, plundered her mouth again. She'd undone his belt buckle before he realized she had, scraping his jeans down urgently, reaching for him.

When she found him, she let out a gasp, and he wanted in her, right then.

But rushing heaven wasn't what he wanted.

He pushed her back against the pillows, slowly undid the soft velour belt of her robe, gently pulled the towel from her head so that the red hair he loved was free. She touched her wet locks uncomfortably, suddenly shy, but he wasn't having that. He drew open her robe, pushing the fabric to either side of her body so that he could look to his heart's content as he tore off his boots and socks.

She pulled at him to hurry him, but he wasn't hurrying. Her nipples had peaked in the cool air, hardening into tantalizing points on top of luscious mounds of white skin. He cupped a breast, one first and then the other, groaning when she gasped as he thumbed a nipple to hardness.

She reached for him again, but he caught her hand, kissing her fingertips. Captured her hand on the bed so that she couldn't reach him. He didn't dare let her touch him— he was far too ready for her, and if she wrapped that small, delicate hand around his shaft, he wasn't going to last for what he really wanted.

And what he really wanted lay bare to his vision. He let his fingers enjoy the path from her hard nipple down the soft skin to her belly button, traced the smoothness of her hips. She was gorgeous—and wet, he realized, hot for him, as his wandering fingers made it at last from the vee downward. Very wet, and with a groan, he traced up and down the tight hidden crevice, enjoying the slickness that was all for him. She squirmed.

"Santana." It was a plea he felt go all the way through him.

"You're beautiful," he murmured, "so beautiful. I could look at you forever."

He could never get tired of Emma like this, bare and vulnerable before him, and yet not near as vulnerable as he was, because he needed her so much. He was crazy about her, for her. There wasn't a moment he didn't think about her, want her.

He bent to kiss the delicate red vee, meaning to convey with his kiss how he felt about her. But when she squirmed, her hand tensing beneath his, he couldn't help himself. He kissed her bud, suckling it. Slipped a finger inside her, and she arched against him, crying out his name.

"Santana!"

He was astonished when she climaxed, hard. It was too fast—he'd wanted to draw her pleasure out. He spread her legs, intending to pleasure her again, but she pulled him onto the bed, throwing him off balance so that he tumbled forward.

"Emma—"

"I need you." She got on top of him, kissed his lips hard, grinding against him.

When she sank onto him, he thought his heart would stop.

"Fuck me," she whispered. "Fuck me, Santana."

He thrust up into her, and she cried out, her hands

digging into his skin. She matched his thrusts, riding him. He desperately tried to hang on, not wanting to come until she did. Needing to feel her pleasure, needing to know he pleased her, he rocked into her hard, nearly passing out when she cried out his name over and over.

His own climax nearly blacked out his brain. If he'd always wondered where he was going to belong on this planet, he didn't wonder any more. Against all odds, he belonged in Emma's arms.

"It should be a crime to want you as much as I do," he said, falling back with a groan. He stared up at the ceiling realizing that the words that had somehow left his mouth were absolutely true. It wasn't just want, either. It was blinding, deep-rooted *need*.

She rolled over and looked at him, propping up on his chest. He felt his heart lurch happily at the familiarity.

"You know, it's not just you."

He raised a brow. "Oh?"

"No. I want you, too."

"Yeah?" He hoped like hell that was true.

"A little." She winked at him. "Maybe."

He looked into her eyes, feeling himself fall deeply into something. Something.

Oh, hell, who was he kidding?

What he'd fallen into was love. "There's no way this ends well."

She kissed him. "Who says it has to end?"

He didn't know what to say to that. His future was murky, his past murkier. Just returning to Star Canyon and leaving the Navy behind had required soul searching. He needed time to process what he'd left behind in the Middle East, brothers he would never see again. It had been a hard job, but he'd been committed to it and the need to serve. He'd expected a transition when he'd returned, but the transition was pretty fucked up. He'd been empty before, now he felt lost somehow. Except when he held Emma. Wasn't that fucked up, too? Latching on to the class geek voted Most Likely to Succeed, when he knew he had dark spaces that might not ever be filled again.

His arms tightened reflexively around her. "The thing is, Emma, I'm pretty broken."

"I'm good at putting things back together."

Of course she couldn't possibly understand, because he didn't even know if he could make it back from the edge of the darkness. His father had spun them into a whole new world of crazy.

"It's okay, Santana. You've warned me. I'm a big girl. You don't have to protect me."

He wanted to believe her so badly, wanted to believe that it would be okay. And when Emma moved on top of him, Santana grabbed her hips and told himself this slice of heaven could last forever.

He'd just never experienced forever before.

• • •

Christmas in the Star Canyon square was beautiful. Ropes of green garlands hung over the windows of the few shops and Mary's restaurant. Red bows adorned every black lamppost. Star Canyon #1 even had a Christmas tree out front, and two wreaths on the doors.

The Magic Wedding Dress shop was dark and lacked

decorations. Some folks had approached Santana to mention that livening it up a little with some holiday spirit might be a good thing. Sierra's grand opening had been canceled. They wanted to know if the store itself was going to die before it ever opened. Sierra's absence had been impossible to ignore—everybody knew instantly that she had left town.

His sister had that effect. By far the most visible and personable of the Darks, she checked in on people, frequented stores, volunteered. She was greatly missed.

"Thanks for agreeing to help me with this," Santana said gruffly, feeling bad that he'd had to drag Emma into his family's issue. "I haven't got the first clue about holiday décor."

"Give me the key. I'll look around, see if Sierra put some stuff in the back. She had to have been thinking of decorating. She was planning her grand opening for the week of Christmas." Emma looked at the brand-new sign that Sierra had been so proud of, and Santana felt a twinge of unease, though he couldn't have said why.

"I'll call her and ask her."

She looked at him. "Have you spoken to her since she left?"

"Cisco had a brief text that she was fine, that she was exploring her new head space with appreciation for solitude."

"That sounds like Sierra."

It did. "Do you mind starting without me?"

Emma opened the door. "Go. You're not needed for this small job. I'll let you know what I find. In the meantime, maybe go hunt up the Captain."

She closed the door, and he heard her lock it, which was smart, since The Magic Wedding Dress shop wasn't ready for visitors. He didn't have to worry about Emma. She was levelheaded, and this area was safe. He dialed Sierra's number, went straight into voice mail. "Sierra, we're digging around looking for your ornaments. This isn't exactly my strong suit, but the town fathers want all the stores holiday-ready. Like Lightning Canyon," he said as an afterthought, hoping to rouse his sister's competitive spirit. Sierra was nothing if not competitive. "Anyway, give us a shout if there's anything you've squirreled away that we should use for your store."

There was no more he could do here. Emma hadn't seemed to require him for this job, and frankly, the less time he spent in his sister's pipe dream, the happier he'd be. Damn Nick Marshall for encouraging something that he had to have known would never happen.

But he couldn't really blame Sierra's meltdown on his cousin. He decided to take Emma's advice and head over to the station, which he'd been avoiding, a fact Emma probably knew. He hadn't been there since he'd returned home. Deployed too far away and in too sensitive of a location, he'd been reached after the accident. After the service for his father. Sonny's body hadn't been recovered. There were a few minor injuries among the firefighters, a collapsed lung, a broken leg at the abandoned building, but Sonny's remains had never been found after the explosion.

The tingle of unease hit him again. He couldn't explain the feeling. If he was honest, he'd think he was holding back a premonition, the split-second warning that had saved him many a time in remote, dangerous locations. Sonny always said that Santana walked with a spirit guardian.

Santana had always hoped so. He needed a spirit guardian. But this wasn't the guardian keeping him safe. No, this unease was merely the soul of a man not wanting to revisit the past and its ghosts.

But it was time.

He walked across to Star Canyon #1, pulling his jacket up to keep the sudden chill off the back of his neck, and walked in, as if he were returning to his home away from home after a long absence.

The passing of time hit him hard as he walked by the familiar equipment, heard the low murmur of voices of men going about their work, saw the shiny red of the two trucks Star Canyon had assiduously budgeted for. He was listening for something, and he suddenly knew what was missing: The boom of his father's voice, talking with his colleagues, encouraging the younger firefighters. They'd looked up to him, and his extensive knowledge. That was the father he'd known. Not the gambler, the man who'd lost the family ranch, the man who inexplicably had adopted five children, cobbling them together as a family who loved each other. Children he'd guided and encouraged to seek education and a higher calling—that was the man Santana had known.

That voice was gone.

And in its place was now a quiet hollow as the gentle memories had been ripped away to a new, unfriendly reality.

Santana forced himself to stay and face his own demons.

"Hey," Tag Murtaugh said, coming in to greet him. Tag was a big, athletic man with dark skin and a ready smile. Santana had heard Sonny say more than once that Tag was one of the station's best they'd had come on in a long time. Tag had gone from "cadet" status to respected leader in record time. "I didn't know you were paying us a visit."

They slapped backs and did the guy thing for a second.

Some of the doubt Santana had felt slipped away. The slight Scottish accent that was embedded in Tag's voice was comforting, too. "How's your father?"

"Dad's good. Spending a lot of time gardening now that he's retired." A shadow passed over his eyes. "I'm sorry as hell about your father, Santana. We tried, we did our best—"

Santana held up a hand to ward off the words. "I know, man. If there was a crew that could have helped Dad, this was the one. Nothing more needs to be said."

Tag nodded. "I don't know, but the word on the down-low is that the captain's been looking at Jack Pearson."

"For arson?" Jack Pearson was the town blight. He was completely unlike his sister, True, who ran the hair salon. Everybody loved True.

Nobody loved Jack Pearson except his sister.

Santana understood that. As far as he was concerned, Sierra hung the moon. Nothing was ever going to change that. Brothers and sisters had a special bond.

"Sheriff Hayden seems to think there was a firebug involved," Tag said. "He's convinced that there was an accelerant out at Mac Callie's place, too, and maybe the same used at the warehouse. It didn't go up on its own." He was sure of that. He hadn't driven out to see the place the biggest fire Star Canyon had ever seen had destroyed. As far as he knew, neither had his brothers.

Sierra had. She'd told them not to go.

His brothers said some nights Sierra woke up, crying out after that visit. Santana figured he had enough demons that he didn't need to stir the little fuckers up any more than they already were.

"Sheriff mentioned he might take a closer look at the

chemicals Kayla Wright's creating out at her lab. That's strictly confidential between you and me, bro."

Santana's eyes widened. "Jenny's sister?" Emma would be devastated. Jenny was one of her best friends. It was a tough call who was her best, Jenny or Sierra. He dared not tell Emma. The secret would hang heavy in his gut, though.

"I thought the good doctor's work is highly monitored by the government and thousands of other agencies, because of terrorism cautions."

"Everything's monitored. Tightly," Tag said. "It's just a hunch the sheriff and some Rangers are working on."

Santana shook his head, unwilling to hear anymore. "They'll get to the bottom of it. I hope."

Tag slapped him on the back again. "They will. I just wanted you to know, none of us will ever forget your father. He was a fine man. Hey, stop by his locker, if you want." Tag left to take his shift, and Santana wandered over to the lockers, seeing at once that Sonny's locker had his photo on it. Some words of respect from his fellow firefighters were written on pieces of paper and closed, taped to the shrine.

With a heavy sigh, Santana opened the locker, making certain he didn't disturb the notes on the outside.

All his father's things were inside, untouched. Tears jumped into his eyes and his throat closed up hard.

A photo in a frame was attached to the inside of the locker door: Sonny and his five kids when they were younger, all together. Happier days. Santana remembered his mother taking the photo. Sonny had been laughing because she said she couldn't hold the camera still enough to take it. Sierra had been young enough that her hair was in tiny pigtails. Cisco and Luke wore boots, scuffed and worn, second-hand, if he recalled correctly. Romero grinned, missing a tooth in front, delighted that the tooth fairy had left him a nickel.

Santana was at the end of the group surrounding their father. Sonny's hand was on his shoulder, squeezing it. Hanging on to him. His father's grip had been strong.

He'd been strong enough to survive many fires, had many saves.

Sonny had known better than anyone that any fire could be the last. You had to live life each day as if you might not get another, Sonny said.

If he were here today, he'd say it again.

His father's smile haunted him, the happy sparkle in his eyes completely belying everything they'd learned at the reading of his will. The man they'd known was not the man he'd been.

Santana closed the locker and left.

• • •

Emma hadn't wanted Santana to stay and hunt decorations for several reasons. One, she didn't need help with such a trivial task. Sierra had been so excited about her store that she surely had stocked something away. Emma felt certain.

Emma flipped on a light and gasped when she saw the reflection of a gown in the mirrors Sierra had put in with such pride. "Well, that won't do," she told the gown. "You scared me half to death. Back into your bag you go." She grabbed the garment bag which was slung on a table. It wasn't like Sierra to leave her prized possessions where dust could fall on them, or critters might make themselves at home in the fabric.

She gazed at the dress, remembering Melly Shelby's touching story Emma's hands warmed at the memory, almost uncomfortably. She dropped the garment bag where it had been lying. "I'll zip you away before I leave. First, ornaments."

The salon itself looked as if it was caught in time, suspended until Sierra finally opened her wonderful shop. And it would be wonderful, Emma thought, touching the velvet tufted chairs grouped around the salon. The room was centered on the mirrors, so that a bride could try on her dream gown, and be the focus of everyone's attention. Emma wondered what it would be like to want to be a bride.

She'd never thought of getting married. Men had asked her out, but the experience of being taken to dinner by people she'd known all her life and who were now beginning to cast their gazes at her in a new light was unsettling. She'd been the class nerd too long to see herself in the way she apparently seemed to her old classmates.

A twinkle caught her eye as she walked into the large storeroom. Boxes were neatly stacked, ordered with different labels. Emma didn't stop to look at the boxes, though she suspected these contained all the things Sierra had collected in the barn at the ranch.

Instead she'd chosen to open a bridal shop, based on a dream.

Sierra didn't believe in dreams. Sierra relied totally on herself.

She spied a twinkle again at the back of the storeroom and edged her way around the boxes to reach it, glad for the bright light in the room.

"What are you doing?" a male voice demanded.

She whirled with a gasp. "Jack Pearson! You scared the shit out of me!"

The tall teenager with the blond, buzzed head and clear green eyes shrugged. "What are you doing? This isn't your store."

Emma felt a sudden tremor of unease. "I'm here because Santana asked me to be here. What are you doing in here?"

He shrugged. "Saw the lights were on."

The lights were always on for the sake of security. Sheriff Lee liked the shops kept lit around the square. She couldn't explain why True Pearson's younger brother bothered her so much. He had a face that was bland and unremarkable. You didn't know what Jack was thinking until he opened his mouth. Some people in the town claimed Jack was a troublemaker, but she'd never seen any evidence of that.

Not that she was taking any chances.

"Thank you for checking on the store, but I would prefer if it you left." Emma frowned. "How did you get in, anyway?" She knew very well she'd locked the door. Santana had insisted on it—though she would have done so anyway.

"The door wasn't locked." Jack shrugged again. "Thought somebody might be stealing something."

"Why would you assume someone was stealing something?"

"Or they might be up to other kinds of trouble."

Suddenly Emma felt very uncomfortable being alone in the back storeroom with him. "Everything's fine. You can leave. I'll tell Santana you checked on the store," she said, hoping he'd feel that his efforts hadn't gone unnoticed and would go.

She was surprised and a little weak when he meekly

turned around and left the shop. The door closed with a whisper, and she flew to lock it, making certain this time to try the handle. It didn't budge, and Emma sank onto one of the velvet chairs to collect her thoughts.

Suddenly, ornament-hunting held little appeal. She didn't want to be in the shop any longer this late at night. There were only two ways into the shop, the front door, and a door at the back for deliveries. Jumping up, she hurried to the back, pulling on the handle.

It opened easily. Emma gasped, slamming it shut, locking it, turning the deadbolt.

Jack had come in from the back. He hadn't known she was in here at all. She glanced around at all the boxes. If these boxes contained the items Sierra had collected over the years, then Jack might have been helping himself, knowing full well that Sierra probably had no catalog system. No one would ever know what, or if, anything was missing. And everyone knew Sierra had left town.

Taking a deep breath to calm herself, Emma glanced toward the back of the stockroom one last time, startled to see a twinkle thrown off the handmade dress. Or at least that's what it looked like. She edged toward the dress, mesmerized. Reaching into the bag, she touched the fabric. Nothing happened, so she drew the gown from its bag and hung it on the rack to inspect it.

Emma wasn't certain anyone would buy this gown, even at a garage sale. It was beautiful, old-fashioned in a lovely way.

She thought about Santana's surprise marriage proposal, which he hadn't mentioned again. She would love to wear this dress to marry Santana.

She pushed the unlikely thought away.

This dress—and shop—were simply magic beans. Sierra had likely borrowed what little money she had for this gown—and maybe even for this crazy idea of a wedding dress shop. Women who married in Star Canyon usually opted for something practical, like a skirt and jacket or a dress, and went to the justice of the peace.

Light music tinkled somewhere, a delicate chime that called to her. Emma smiled at the dress. "I believe in magic," she said, "but your owner doesn't. If you're going to bring her good luck, you'd better get on it." She smiled at the fancy of her thoughts. "I'm going to call you the magic beans dress."

Silly to be talking to a gown. She was just occupying her mind. And she told herself the sudden urge to try the gown on was ridiculous, a waste of time.

She had no reason to need a dress for a wedding. She and Santana were the farthest thing from a couple.

Her deepest secret that she'd never shared with anyone, though, was that she was in love with him. Had been forever.

If there was anyone who needed magic, Emma supposed, it was her.

Besides, who would know?

She reached for the gown.

CHAPTER FOURTEEN

The front door unlocked and opened, and Santana walked in, his face strained. "Hi."

"Hi," she said, putting the dress back on the rack, glad he hadn't caught her trying it on. He took a chair, sighing tiredly. "Did you go to the station?"

"I did."

She went to him, and he pulled her into his lap. He held her against his chest, and she nestled there, content to be in his arms. She remembered how difficult it had been to go into her father's room and clean his things out. Sometimes that wistful nostalgia even caught her at the clinic, when she was among his favorite patients. "It was hard, wasn't it?"

"Yeah."

He wasn't going to say anything else, but Emma understood now that she'd been lost in a fantasy. She wanted more from him than he could give at the moment. Or maybe ever.

"Did you find Sierra's ornaments?"

That had been the last thing on her mind once she'd seen the gown. "I'll buy some," she said brightly. "Tomorrow."

"Thanks."

She didn't know what else to say. He was quieter than he normally was. Something was definitely wrong, but she sensed he didn't want to talk about it. "Jack Pearson was in the store tonight."

"Why?" Santana asked, his tone sharp.

"I think he uses the back door to ramble around the shop."

"Why would he want to hang out in a wedding dress shop?"

"I have no idea." Emma shrugged as they locked up and left the store, slowly walking across to the Midnight Grill. "He startled me, and I didn't think to ask too many questions. I was pretty focused on getting him to leave so I could lock the back door."

Santana's hand shot out, capturing hers. "He didn't do anything to upset you? Frighten you?"

"No, not really." Emma decided to skip the fact that he'd actually creeped her out. "I just wasn't sure why he was there."

"Probably because he loafs around town with nothing better to do than get in trouble, while True does all the work."

"True thinks her brother hung the stars."

"He didn't. I'll talk to him."

• • •

"You have to go way back when the town was first founded," Mary told them as she handed them menus they knew by heart, "to know that the Pearsons have always been slightly weird. Different, if you know what I mean."

Santana had asked Mary if she'd seen Jack hanging around the square, and particularly Sierra's shop.

"Their families came from California," Mary said, "and before that, Australia. Came here with just about nothing, the early Pearsons did. They never forgot that, either. Felt like they didn't fit in. The only one that never drove me straight up a tree is True, but then she's from the Stafford family, and the Staffords are good people. Never really understood why True's mother married a Pearson. Angel Stafford was a good woman. Think she could have done better, if you ask me," Mary whispered. "Now what'll you have?"

They ordered without looking at the menu, and Mary left.

"Are you worried about Jack?"

"I'll mention to Sheriff Lee that he was in the shop. He shouldn't be getting into businesses on the square."

"Don't you think it was a one-off maybe, since Sierra's shop is empty?"

"It's full of her stuff. She's got all kinds of Sierra booty squirreled away in there. For all we know, Jack's been selling it. That wedding dress you were holding—"

"Putting away," she said.

"Right." He winked at her. "I wasn't suggesting you were going to try it on."

She had been about to do just that when he'd returned. Emma looked at him. "So what about it?"

"I guess Jack Pearson could sell something like that, for example," he went on, apparently done with teasing her for the moment, for which she was grateful.

"I guess," she said thoughtfully. "I don't know what he was doing. He said he was checking on me, to see why someone was in the shop. I wondered if maybe he was planning on grabbing some of Sierra's stuff, but I suppose a single wedding dress could disappear just as easily."

His hand covered hers suddenly, warming her. "You could talk me into a private viewing, by the way." He raised a brow. "It's hard for a man to concentrate in a brightly-lit shop when anyone can walk by and look in the window, but I promise you, something about seeing you holding that dress made me want to…"

"Try it on yourself?" Emma teased.

"Babe, you're asking for a spanking later."

Mary set drinks on the table, waved to some newcomers, and dashed off.

"I'll look forward to that," Emma said demurely.

"A spanking?"

"If you don't lose your nerve," she said, all sweetness.

"My nerve is not what you have in mind, I'm pretty certain." He massaged her fingers with his, then pulled away—as if he'd suddenly realized he was acting like they were more than just friends.

He sipped his beer as if they hadn't gotten lost in the momentary teasing about the wedding gown. Which they had, and it had felt right. Emma knew it.

"Don't back out now, big boy," she said softly. "I can feel you trying to, but I promise you'll like spanking me more than your wildest fantasies have ever allowed you to imagine."

• • •

Santana's breath hitched hard. Heat flared inside him, ran all over his body. She'd read his mind about backing away from her.

She was deliberately luring him—and he liked it. Against his better judgment that eluded him every time she got near him, and every time he thought about her, fantasized about her. Hell, resistance was futile, because sometimes, he forgot why he was resisting.

So since the lady was offering, a nice gentle, *thorough* spanking it was going to be. And then, he was going to make love to her the way she deserved: inch by slow scorching inch, all night long.

• • •

Nick sat in his penthouse overlooking Uptown, staring out the huge windows and seeing nothing. He was barely aware of the three couples circulating around him, and the sophisticated brunette who was trying to engage him in conversation. Her hand was on his trouser leg, warming his thigh.

His mind, goddamn it, was on a blue-tufted pixie of a girl with a sassy mouth and saucy personality back in Star Canyon. Or wherever she was.

His not-cousin. He wanted a family, a real one, so badly it hurt. His father, damn his mercenary and greedy hide, had handed him exactly what he wanted, in the most roundabout way. The last thing on his father's mind was cementing family relations. He was interested in cementing power and the fortunes of the Marshall name. Politics was calling, and nothing said salt-of-the-earth more than a huge ranch.

Sonny Dark's misfortune had been all gain for the Marshall side.

Only his father hadn't calculated that Nick lacked the necessary ingredient for going in for the tiger-like kill. And Nick didn't need more money or land, and he wasn't interested in politics.

He was interested in family.

The twist was, Sierra was the last thing on earth he should ever want in a woman. The very last thing. But she sure as hell was no sister figure to him. They had no blood, no common background, had never shared a roof, except in Lightning Canyon, and even then he'd actually slept in his damn car.

He had never wanted a woman the way he wanted Sierra.

And she wasn't interested in him, not one bit. Nor anyone else, as far as he could tell. He shouldn't be thinking about her—not a thousand times a day—especially when there was a beauty right beside him, her hand edging dangerously close to her target. But he wasn't going to sleep with her. It wouldn't help.

He'd become infected somehow with the Dark eccentricities, and all he could think of was a woman with tats and a face piercing he shouldn't want at all.

But she'd invited him into her bed. Oh, she'd fibbed a little and told him there were two beds in the room at Miss Sugar's—but there'd only been one. She'd been more subtle about her invitation than the brunette who'd just scooted herself up against his side, pressing into him to get his wandering attention.

He couldn't forget Sierra's invitation.

She was right. He was a boring chickenshit, because a man

who wasn't a boring chickenshit would have jumped right into bed with her and enjoyed all the sass he could handle.

And thinking about that was the first time he'd had an erection all evening. Disappointing the brunette—what was her name?—he got up and went to pour himself a whiskey.

• • •

"Tell his royal highness to get his dumb butt back here or we're going to take the ranch over like squatters," Romero said. "How does he think cattle and horses get cared for? Magic elves?"

"I agree," Cisco said. "Whatever made Nick go off, tell him to fix it. Does he really pay you?"

"Just got a check," Santana said mildly. It had been generous, more generous that the job was probably worth. Maybe a little guilt money. "You sprung yourselves on him, remember?"

"We have no formal offer of employment," Luke said. "We are, in fact, squatters. I say we break into the house and live life like we used to."

"I think that would be against the law." Santana wondered himself if Nick planned to come back, or if he was going to be more of a hands-off owner. "He didn't say much to me when he left. It was Sierra who moved you guys in on him. Be thankful for that."

"And meanwhile, has anyone heard from Sierra lately?" Cisco checked his phone.

"I saw a credit card charge in Montana." Santana knew that would stir up his brothers, and he'd been none too pleased himself.

"You're tracking her credit cards?" Luke stopped what he was doing. "She's going to be pissed if she figures that out."

"I'm not proud of it, but I was getting worried." He leaned against a sawhorse. "Looked like she stopped to buy food for Joe." He still couldn't believe she'd taken his dog. That dog she said he needed to keep his head from lodging up his butt.

Maybe that ship had sailed.

"If we know where she is, why don't we go talk to her?" Romero demanded.

"Because nobody dragged me home when I left, and nobody impeded your travels when the three of you wanted to hit the white sands of Mexico." Which was another reason why he loved thinking about Emma about a hundred times a day: She was steady, she was sane. She had her clinic, and that was always going to be her touchstone, right here, in Star Canyon. He didn't have to worry about her going off on an expedition to find herself.

Although finding her wearing the wedding gown last night had been a shocker. To be honest, after his visit to the station, he'd been so screwed up he'd been ready to put an end to their relationship, jump in his truck, and hit the highway. See if he could outrun the pain.

Then he'd seen Emma looking like a goddess, and everything inside him had rushed to life. Even now, he wished she was here. It was staggering how much he needed her.

She said she wasn't expecting anything from him, but that wasn't fair. Emma Glass deserved a man who was a stayer, a man who would never leave, a man who would wake her up every morning with a hot kiss and some hotter lovemaking.

"So, what's up with you and Dr. Glass?" Romero asked.

His brother lounged near an empty stall. "Somebody said they saw her trying on wedding dresses. Something you need to tell us?"

"I wasn't trying on wedding gowns," Santana said, "why are you asking me?"

"Town grapevine says the two of you were locked in a hot-and-heavy," Luke said, "which we neither confirmed nor denied. But we did wonder."

Cisco grinned. "It's good to see you happy, bro."

"Now, wait a minute," Santana said, "when wasn't I happy?"

His brothers guffawed, leaving the barn. "Hey! I've been happy my whole life! Nothing's changed!"

They didn't turn around. "I'm a ray of sunshine," Santana muttered to himself. "What the hell do they know about my happiness?"

• • •

Emma closed up the clinic and drove to the small library on the square, which was run by Honey Martin, Captain Phil's estranged wife. Phil and Honey lived in separate houses, but Emma had high hopes that one day they'd reconcile.

In the meantime, she wanted to do some research on supernatural phenomena, and though their library was small, Honey managed to collect some gems over the years. The library was her passion. She even had a couple of free "tiny" libraries she'd scattered around the more far-flung parts of Star Canyon, so that folks who couldn't get into town often had something to read. Where there was a person, there was a reader, Honey liked to say.

Honey was also Star Canyon's resident expert on woo-woo—that being Honey's label for the constant investigation she liked to do into what others privately called silly. Or mystical. Or communing with the spirits and ghosts. Honey just let everybody tease her and went on about her business with a smile. Those who believed in otherworldly matters thought Honey was an angel. Tonight, Emma was looking for guidance, and here in Honey's sanctuary, she hoped she'd find it.

"Hello!" Honey called as soon as Emma walked in the wide doors of the library. "Come for a gossip, or a book?"

"Both. Maybe some advice."

"If it's relationship advice, I'm the last one you should ask." Honey smiled. Her silvery-gray hair shone under the hanging lamps over the circulation desk. "I hear you've been hanging out with a certain Navy SEAL."

"Some," Emma said, hedging, and Honey laughed.

"What can I help you with?"

Everything that had happened in Lightning Canyon had stayed on her mind since that night. The discussion about ghosts. Mystical wedding gowns that twinkled. She hadn't imagined that. Sierra had recovered from her fever quickly in Lightning Canyon—and she had a feeling it had less to do with Miss Sugar's homeopathy than something else. "What do you know about supernatural occurrences?" Emma asked, feeling slightly embarrassed for asking.

"That they happen every day. What variety are you curious about?" Honey pulled a book toward her, opening the well-worn tome to a spot with a wisteria-printed bookmark inside. "They happen all the time. Let me lock up. It's closing time. Read that page and see if it answers the questions you have."

"Over time a thing becomes a talisman if enough people imbue it with their belief system," Emma read. Honey turned off a few of the overhead lights in the large room and drew a lamp closer to Emma's and her seat. "A thing can be wished into being," Honey said. "But your question is, if something happens because of magic, is it real. Or did you just want it that bad that you made it happen."

"That's exactly what I want to know," Emma said, surprised. She thought back to that night in the wedding shop, and Melly Shelby's gown. The gown hadn't held any mystical powers for Miss Shelby. And no wedding dress, enchanted or otherwise, was going to solve Honey and the Captain's issue that kept them apart—whatever it was—nor would a simple dress and a good fairy tale change anything for Mary. So why had she seen what she had? "Have you ever had a vision?"

Honey smiled. "One doesn't necessarily share their visions freely, do they? Especially if one is the steady, make-no-waves librarian."

Emma looked at her. "So you do believe in visions."

Honey nodded decisively. "I certainly do."

"I mean, outside of drinking or taking pharmaceuticals."

Honey giggled. "Why in the world would I confuse the two?" She grew serious. "A true vision changes a person. You never forget it, but more importantly, it changes your life."

Emma's breath caught. "Why?"

"Because a true vision makes you want to deserve it," Honey said. "You know that's your way, so to speak. If it's not a true vision, it sort of melts away. It's hard for people to change, so sometimes only a real vision will make it happen."

Sierra didn't believe in enchantment, claimed she didn't believe in anything. Sierra was looking for something—or she'd be here in Star Canyon right now. The dress and the shop had just been a momentary illusion of permanence. Sierra didn't want the shop, the dress—or Nick.

Emma claimed she wasn't looking for a permanent man in her life, either. The clinic kept her plenty busy, at least that's what she'd always told herself.

But had she dreamed Santana into her arms? Because honestly, that's what it felt like, a wonderful dream she never wanted to wake from.

"Maybe I was looking for something and I never realized it," Emma said slowly.

"You mean Santana." Honey nodded. "And secretly you're wondering if he's too damaged to go the distance. If you're wrong to get your hopes up. But you feel magic, anyway, when you're together. It's hard to believe, isn't it?" She sighed. "I can see where your belief systems might be challenged. I would certainly change mine if a hunky fellow like him came into my life. And you've always been the steadfast sort, from your childhood." Honey smiled wistfully. "But it's okay to believe in love, Emma. When the sheriff proposed to me, I would have gone to the ends of the earth to be with him."

Emma was stunned. "You live in the same town, and you're not with him now, Honey," she said, as gently as possible.

"One never knows. People change over time, don't they?"

"I don't think I do," Emma said, thinking that if Santana

was ever hers, she wouldn't want their love to change. She'd want it to grow brighter, burn hotter.

"Oh, but you have." Honey's face was serene with wise understanding. "You're changing because you've fallen in love."

"How do I know it's real? And that I just didn't want it so much I made it happen?" Emma asked, feeling stupid for having to ask, and scared that the beautiful thing that she and Santana had might somehow slip away.

"Because I'm guessing you've had a vision."

"I did. I thought maybe I was crazy," Emma said. "But it's stayed with me and every day, I'm more convinced that my heart belongs to Santana. I don't know if he feels the same." She shrugged. "And what woman doesn't see twinkles and sparkles when she sees a wedding gown?"

The second she said it, Emma knew she wasn't going to convince Honey or herself that she wasn't madly in love with Santana. It had nothing to do with weddings or gowns or if they ever even talked about a serious relationship between them. She was in love with him, and her heart knew it was real.

No matter what happened, she was going to have to throw caution to the wind and admit that she was mad for a certain Navy SEAL.

"You're a practical woman, Emma. A daddy's girl." Honey smiled. "You know your father was a fine man. And when he passed away unexpectedly, I watched you suffer. You bore it silently, and stepped into his shoes. You're not crazy, you're just beginning to understand the magic that is available to us on earth, if we allow it to come into our lives.

It's hard sometimes to accept that there are supernatural blessings available to us after we've suffered a loss."

"I guess I just needed to know that I wasn't believing in something that wasn't there." She took a deep breath. "I guess I'm looking for answers. Thank you for helping me find them."

"Well," Honey said, closing her book with the pretty bookmark in it, "the only way to really find out the answer you need is to ask, isn't it?"

Ask Santana if he wanted a relationship with her, just the two of them. Long-term.

Long-term was the problem. Santana didn't know anything long-term. His whole life had been upended when Sonny hadn't made it out of the biggest fire Star Canyon had ever seen.

"What do you think happened the night Sonny died, Honey?"

"Well, not that the captain talks about such things with me, when we do talk," Honey said slowly, "but I have an idea that we're going to learn surprising things about that night. We have so many new folks in town, you know. The artist's colony has been a good thing for Star Canyon. But it's brought other folks in as well. It's been a lot of change for our little town."

Which meant there was precious little new information yet that could help the Darks.

Rapping on the door made both ladies jump. They could see Santana's large frame through the glass door, and Emma's heart instantly leaped.

"There's your man." Honey got up. "You know," she said, "trusting a vision sometimes means walking through a door to a new and unexpected place. But you have to open the door to find the answers you seek."

Emma sat still as Honey gave her a kind smile and went to let Santana in. "You gave two ladies quite a start, young man."

"I saw Emma's truck. Though I'd stop by to rescue you, Honey."

Emma watched him walk in, big, handsome, beautiful, mouthwatering, oh-my-God sexy, and wondered how she could ever back away from a man she'd loved almost all her life.

She couldn't. No matter what he had going on in his life, she was going to have to wait to find out if the vision she'd had meant anything.

She did believe in magic—and Honey was correct: Once you'd had a vision, you wanted to believe in it, deserve it, wish it into your life. Get closer to it, again and again and again.

And that was how the vision had changed her: She was going to walk on the wild side, put her heart out there.

For love. For Santana.

And hope she didn't get burned.

CHAPTER FIFTEEN

Santana awakened in the night, his heart racing, his head thick with blackness. Holy fuck, where was he? He heard yells, maybe rockets, gunfire. Thick smoke surrounded him. He hunkered down, reached for his Sig, couldn't find it.

Something warm and soft shifted near him. A small hand moved to his rod, stroking him. Some of the darkness shifted. He was in bed with Emma. The adrenaline changed to a different kind of fire as she warmed him, teasing him into hot hardness.

"It's okay," she whispered. "You're in Star Canyon. You're at my house."

Caught in the nightmare, he must have tensed, maybe yelled.

His heart still raced uncontrollably. The blackness hadn't subsided. He tried to concentrate on Emma's magic touch, letting it chase off the nightmare. Heal him.

"Make love to me, Santana," she said urgently, and he did the only thing he could at such a sweet request.

He rolled over, buried himself deep inside her. She

clung to his back, her legs locked around his thighs, drawing him in, urging him faster, *more*.

His throat locked up. She kissed him, drawing his mouth down to hers. Her kisses hungrily claimed him, and he drove inside her relentlessly, her gasps against his lips a salve for the tornado threatening to overwhelm him and destroy his life. The tornado was determined to steal everything he had, curse everything he wanted—but he wasn't going to let the darkness win.

No. Every damn thing—starting with this hot, beautiful woman who seemed to want to be with him, no matter how ugly his scars—had to be his.

He couldn't survive without her.

* * *

Santana thought about taking his brothers with him to the monstrous shell of a burned-out building that stood far from town, a scar against the vast land surrounding it, but he decided against it. This was his journey. They'd come out here when they were ready.

He was ready, as much as he ever could be. He'd visited the grave, of course, but this was where Sonny's spirit had departed its earthly existence. Parking his truck, Santana got out, surprised that he could still smell an acrid tang on the air. This had once been the lifeblood of Star Canyon, a giant warehouse where local cotton, corn, and other goods were stored for market. Cattle were also brought to market here. The hub of Star Canyon had been used by Lightning Canyon and several other small towns, an adjunct vein for farm and ranch commerce.

Sonny would have considered it his duty, no matter what structure or situation was in need, to serve.

Santana felt deep in his soul that so much of what he and his siblings had learned about Sonny after his death was somehow a lie, or at least a harsh variation of the truth. The Sonny Dark he knew as a father and later as a friend, had not been a gambler, a loser hooked on life's temptations. It just didn't square.

And once he realized that, he was free. He still grieved, but his father wouldn't want them to live in the past. He'd been well aware what the path of a firefighter meant.

He walked into what had been the warehouse's four walls, now simply a shell sprawling under a cold dark sky. It was just a few days until Christmas, and without Sierra around, there wasn't a decoration at their rental house. They hadn't decorated the Dark family home, either, and Nick probably didn't care if there even was so much as a Christmas tree at his ranch.

It was time for Nick to pull his head out of his ass. He rang him up.

"Nick Marshall."

"How long are you planning to cower?" Santana demanded.

"What makes you think I am?" Nick shot back.

"You're not here, are you? I knew you were a lightweight, but I never imagined you could get done in a week."

"Ten days. I was there ten days."

Santana looked at the earth beneath his feet. There was still a burnt tinge to the dirt, but stray shoots of green poked through the earth. "You hide out in Dallas for as long as you need."

"Thanks."

Santana snorted at the curtness in his tone. "So, if my brothers are working out here with me, you should be, too."

"I'm not a farmer."

Santana decided not to explain that they weren't farmers, either. The important thing was making Nick understand that he was copping out, and find out why. "Decided that, did you? My sister too much for you?"

Nick cleared his throat. "Did you just call to harass me?"

"That, and to offer you a business proposition you might be interested in." He looked at the burned-out structure yawing to the sky, somehow undefeated by the fire. "You're a hot shit investor, aren't you?"

Nick was silent.

"Or was it your father who was the hot shit investor? The one who bilked my father out of his home and possessions?" He eyed the empty land that stretched as far as the eye could see. "You're not intending to solely live off the inheritance of your father's misdeeds, are you?"

"What do you want, Santana?" Nick growled.

"Come spend Christmas dinner with us," Santana said.

Nick didn't reply.

"That's what you wanted, wasn't it? Holiday dinner with family? So I'm asking."

"None of you are my family. I tried to make you that, but then I realized it was a bad proposition, a business deal that wouldn't work."

"So what? You're going to sell the ranch?"

"Not yet," Nick said with a sigh.

"So you still have a place to park your privileged ass. Come out. We'll break into the family home before you get here and set everything up."

"No need to go smashing windows. I left the key with Emma."

Santana was stunned. "She didn't tell me."

"Because she's a good woman, Santana. She knows you better than you know yourself. She said you'd ask when you were ready. And it sounds like you're coming to terms with the past."

"And you? When do you do that?"

"Oh, that won't be for a long goddamn time," Nick said. "I'll see you on Christmas Eve. I'll bring the booze and cigars. We'll probably need them."

"Nothing too fancy. We can't afford to get soft around here."

"Bite me, cousin," Nick said politely. "Thank you for the phone call." He hung up.

"Always a pleasure," Santana said cheerfully, not offended at all.

He shoved his phone in his pocket and walked to his truck. It wasn't over, the past wasn't put to rest. But he was looking forward to the future, and he hadn't for so long.

Most of all, he looked forward to a future with Emma.

He had a stop to make before he found his way home.

• • •

"Oh, she's beautiful!" Emma gazed into the cage at the very delicate, sweet-throated lovebird inside. "Where did you find her?"

"In Lightning Canyon." He grinned, pleased with himself. "That house where Sierra bought the wedding dress had a woman who was in charge of the estate sale, remember?"

"Yes."

He nodded. "I told her I was looking for a lovebird. I knew you'd said your father had bought yours there. Apparently, somebody in Lightning Canyon breeds them, and they had this one for sale. Her name is Beauty."

"She *is* a beauty!" Emma was delighted. She took the cage from him. "Thank you so much. My other bird has been mourning."

She gently put the cage on a table, reaching in to take Beauty carefully out. "There you go," she said, placing the bird next to the lonely lovebird. The two birds studied each other for a moment, their heads tilting, their eyes bright.

Suddenly, Emma's original lovebird hopped close to its new friend. Santana stood behind her, watching, casually moving his hand onto her shoulder. Emma's heart expanded at his touch, and the unexpected gift. Her eyes misted. "That was easy. I wasn't sure how they would take to each other." She looked up at Santana, closing the cage door. "I'm truly touched. Thank you."

He drew her into his arms. "Anything to see you smile." Her smile—damn, the bad days were easier just knowing he had Emma's smile to look forward to. It was the one thing in life he knew he never wanted to live without: Her and that damn sexy smile of hers.

He held her tight, and she tucked her chin underneath his. Santana closed his eyes as Emma's arms slid up his back, drawing them together.

"Emma."

She looked up at him. "Yes?"

He cleared his throat, suddenly nervous. "The night you were at Sierra's shop, and you were holding that dress—"

"You thought I was picking out the dress for my big

day," she said, her eyes crinkling with laughter. "I was pretty embarrassed that you caught me holding it up to me."

"I don't know about that. But I knew it would look good on you." Right then, he'd known what he hadn't dared to hope before.

She smiled. "Don't worry. You're safe."

Safe? He didn't want to be safe anymore. He wanted to experience life, all the heat, all the cold, the light, the dark. With her.

"I don't suppose you'd care to put up with me for the long term."

"The long term?"

"Yeah." Santana ran a thumb along her lower lip. "Like maybe forever. I don't have much to offer, but—"

She stopped his words with a kiss. "You're offering what I want, and that's you. The answer's yes."

"Yes?" For some reason he was astonished, gratitude swamping him.

"Yeah. I'll move you and Joe in here."

"I don't know when Joe's coming back. Sierra hijacked my damn dog."

"She'll be back, and he'll be back. In the meantime, I have something to give you, for the long term."

"Yeah?" He allowed her to draw him down the hall. "I hope it's a naked beauty named Emma."

She laughed. Sat him on her bed. Turned to her dresser, and took something from a box. Handed him a key.

"Nick told me to give this to you when you were ready to go home."

"Home?"

"To your family home."

"It's his place now."

"Yes." She nodded. "But he said there was only one person who would stick around through thick and thin to help him. And that you deserved to be able to use your family house when you wanted to."

His throat choked up. He pocketed the key. "He's not altogether an asshole."

She smiled. "He's right, you know. You're the one that sticks around through thick or thin." She kissed him. "I love that about you, Santana Dark. I've loved you all my life, from the first time you sneaked a kiss from me. Notice it was the last kiss you ever had to sneak. All the other kisses we've shared were meant to be. You and I are two parts of the same. Honey convinced me it's a little bit of magic, and maybe that's true." She took a deep breath. "But I know in my heart that I'm in love with you, no matter what happens next."

"God, I love you," he said, his voice rough with emotion. "Thank you for healing a broken man." It was true. He'd come home a shell, but he was whole now.

He kissed her, pulling her down to the bed with him, hungrier for her than ever. Gus and Bean had followed them in and were lying beside the bed. The Persian cat stared down from a bookshelf, and the lovebirds made sweet musical sounds in the other room. Santana smiled as he held Emma close, filled with heat and love when she touched her lips to his, joining them.

Nothing had ever been so right than at this moment.

And this moment was forever.

It was so good to be home.

Lightning Source UK Ltd.
Milton Keynes UK
UKOW02f0938020816

279755UK00004B/194/P